EILEEN DREYER

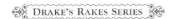

DRAKE'S RAKES SERIES

MISS FELICITY'S DILEMMA

MISS FELICITY'S DILEMMA
Drake's Rakes Series
PUBLISHED BY Eileen Dreyer
Copyright © 2019 by Eileen Dreyer

This is a work of fiction. Names, characters, places and incidents are either the product of the author's imagination or are used fictitiously, and any resemblance to actual persons, living or dead, business establishments, events or locales is entirely coincidental.

Printed in the USA.

Cover Design and Interior Format

For all my readers who patiently waited.

CHAPTER I

1815

IT WAS MISS FELICITY CHAMBERS' considered opinion that more time needed to be spent cleaning beneath beds. She came to this conclusion when the urge to sneeze overtook her as she crouched under the bed of her host, her heart pounding and her eyes squeezed shut.

"You haven't seen her?" a voice rumbled above her.

"I've been looking for *you*," answered the sultry tones of a woman.

A *very* sultry woman. Felicity wished she had the knack for sounding so interesting, rather like she thought a siren might sound when calling sailors to their doom. Sadly, she merely sounded like the new teacher of piano and deportment at Miss Manville's Academy for Superior Girls she was. Well, that she had been before the surprise correspondence had come from the man who was standing four feet from her twitching nose. Lord Flint Bracken.

Flint, Felicity thought with a scowl. *What kind of self-respecting duke named his son after quartz?*

Shouldn't his name be Reginald, or Cyril? But then, from the sound of his voice, she doubted very much that he resembled a Cyril of any kind.

"It was my father's request," he was saying, sounding bored. "Bring the chit here and tell her of the bequest."

Felicity almost bumped her head on the underside of the bed. *Bequest?* Her eyes popped open. *What was he talking about?* Who would leave her anything? She had no one but the other teachers at the academy and the few classmates she still kept in touch with from boarding school. She doubted she would even hear from the family for whom she governessed. Her tenure had not been a stellar success, no matter how much she had loved her pupil.

As for the Brackens, the name was familiar, but then, she had attended school with girls of some of the highest families. And since arriving here, she had seen only a variety of servants. If she had seen anyone else in the last four days—or if any of the servants except the head groom, who only conversed of horses, had deigned to speak to her—she might not have begun searching rooms for evidence of why she had been summoned. She might have stayed out of this room in particular.

"Once I find her," he was saying, his voice now a purr that seemed to thrum right through her, "you and I can continue our own…explorations."

A pair of pink satin slippers crossed Felicity's field of vision, topped by a glimpse of delicate ankles, just the kind she would imagine to be attached to the feet that filled those slippers. Felicity closed her eyes again, as if it would keep her better hidden.

The price of those shoes alone humiliated her. She didn't belong in the same house with those shoes much less the very costly silk dress that matched them.

At least her nose had stopped burning.

Something was going on above her. Something she was certain she had no business witnessing, even with her eyes closed. She heard murmurs and the rustle of fabric, and then, finally, a throaty feminine chuckle.

It wasn't until she heard the door close that she breathed a sigh of relief. Time to escape unnoticed.

"Aren't you growing cramped under there?" Lord Flint suddenly asked.

Felicity's eyes flew open to find an upside-down face where the boots had been. Her heart dropped like a stone.

"Not at all," she said, proud at how composed she sounded. "I am quite petite. But you really should have someone sweep under here. The dust balls are the size of wolfhounds."

He reached a hand under the bed. For a moment Felicity just stared at it, unable to move. Even in the shadows it was a beautiful hand, with long, elegant fingers and a strong wrist. And she noticed beautiful hands. She was also, after all, the substitute art teacher.

"I'm getting a crick in my neck," Lord Flint growled, wiggling his fingers.

Felicity gave up and took hold. And gasped. It felt as if she'd been rubbing her stockinged feet on the carpet on a cold winter's day and gotten a shock. She had heard of such a thing, of course, in every Minerva Press novel she had ever secreted under her pillow. But she had always thought it a literary device. A myth.

That was no myth tingling up her arm.

Before she had a chance to do more than stare at the offending member, Lord Flint grasped her tightly and pulled her out from under the bed. She came out in a tangle of arms and legs, dragging dust after her.

How mortifying, she thought, brushing madly at her sensible gray kerseymere skirts.

"Er...."

She looked up and forgot what she was going to say. She forgot her name.

He was beautiful. Tall and lean and russet-haired, with eyes the color of spring leaves and a humorous cant to his mouth. Chiseled features, square shoulders, slim hips. Hard and sharp as quartz.

Suddenly his name wasn't so funny.

He was brushing at the front of his hair. Felicity frowned. What was he doing? His hair was perfect, thick and well-cut, with just a little curl to make him look a bit mischievous. He shot a pointed look at the top of her head. Instinctively she brushed at her crown and came away with another shower of dust.

"See what I mean?" she demanded, feeling the unlovely red of a blush creep up her cheeks. "You need to speak to your housekeeper."

He didn't look particularly upset. "Do you always hide under beds?"

She couldn't quite meet his gaze. She kept brushing as if the dust hadn't all been quite vanquished. "Only when I am caught in the wrong place."

"And you were in the wrong place because?"

But she had lost her train of thought again. Turning around, she crouched back down. When she had been brushing dust off her bodice, she'd realized she was missing something. The locket little Mary Lassiter had bestowed on her upon leaving her post as Mary's governess. It was nothing much, something Mary said she'd picked up at a county fair for Felicity's birthday, probably pinchbeck. But it was Felicity's only piece of jewelry.

His voice rumbled over her head. "I beg your . . ."

But she didn't answer. On her hands and knees, she pushed her head back under the bed.

There it was, caught on the bed leg. She must have snagged it when she'd been pulled out. Gently disconnecting the chain from the bed frame, she edged back out and knelt on the floor, the chain draped over her fingers, the oval metal gleaming dully in the light.

She fought an odd tightness in her throat. The catch was broken. Well, of course it was. Her only piece of jewelry, her only memory of a little girl who had come looking for her every morning to share some new discovery when no one else would talk to her, and it was broken. And she lacked the funds to fix it. Why should she expect anything else?

"What is that?" his lordship asked, his hand out again.

Felicity instinctively clenched her own hand around the locket. "Nothing." Pocketing the necklace, she took his hand and let him help her back to her feet. "A locket I wear. I must have caught it." She brushed her dress out again. "You were speaking of something."

There was a short pause, as if he wasn't ready to accept her answer. In the end, though, he moved on. "I was asking why you were someplace you weren't supposed to be."

That got her eyes up. "Because I was forced out of my place of employment—"

"Forced? No one forced you. It was a request."

She scowled up at him. "A duke's son may see it as a request. The headmistress of a girls' academy that relies on the good will of the aristocracy takes it as a royal command. I hadn't even time to pack a trunk before I was hustled into that great traveling barge you call a coach and driven twelve hours to this place, where I have been locked up for four days without explanation or company."

He frowned. "Don't be absurd. You weren't locked up. You were free to go at any time."

She tilted her head, becoming quite impatient with the direction of the conversation. Her ankle hurt from where she'd had to bend it to fit under the bed, her necklace was broken, and she was hungry. And this absurd man was standing here telling clankers. "And how was I supposed to do that? I'm not even certain where we are."

"Outside Gloucester, of course."

Of course. She waited in silence. He seemed to be assessing her, his features creased, as if she were as big a puzzle to him as he was to her.

"Well?" she finally demanded, hands on hips. "Why am I here?"

Now he really did look confused. "Did no one tell you?"

"No! I have spent four days wandering this

drafty pile with no company but the head groom and the kitchen cat, both of which are singularly uncommunicative. So, if you do not mind, please tell me why a penniless teacher would receive a summons from the Duke of Lynden, or for the love of all that is holy, send me home. I have classes to teach. If I am not there to do it, they will be given to someone else, and I cannot afford to let that happen."

He was smiling again, as if he knew the biggest joke in the world. Felicity was on the verge of screaming.

"You *are* Miss Felicity Chambers?" he asked.

"Yes, of course. Since you have not bothered to introduce yourself, may I assume you are Lord Flint Bracken?"

His expression froze a bit. "Rather forward for a teacher, aren't you?"

"Rather out of patience and desirous of my luncheon, my lord."

And much preferring to be carrying on this conversation anywhere but right next to this gentleman's bed. But she couldn't tell him that. That *would* be too forward.

"A luncheon you will enjoy in your room," he said.

It was Felicity's turn to look skeptical. "Because?"

She had to admit that there was some enjoyment to seeing such a self-possessed man actually blush. "Because I had not been told you were already here, so I brought company."

She nodded. "Ah. The siren."

He stared. "The what?"

She made a general motion toward the door.

"The lady in pink."

"Er..." He actually turned that way, as if to reacquaint himself with the woman. "Yes. And others."

Finally, her visit threatened to become interesting. "A bit warm for the likes of me, are they?"

This time she got a full-blown scowl, with dark brows almost meeting in the center of his forehead. "That is not for you to ask, young lady."

She couldn't help it. She chuckled. "I am not thirteen, my lord. If you wish me to stay away, I will be delighted. As long as I am assured of a few of Cook's brambleberry tarts, of course."

"Extortion now?"

"Until I can get an answer, yes. There should be some reason for me to stay."

This time he chuckled, his features suddenly easing, his hands on his hips. His *slim* hips, Felicity couldn't help noticing. His blasted elegant hands.

"Oh, there are reasons for you to stay."

She sighed. "And am I ever to find out what they are?"

"In time."

"No," she retorted, finally losing what patience she had left. He was too distracting for her own good, and she knew better than to believe in miracles or myths. "I think not. Either I know or I go. Now that I have learned where we are, it should be possible to find transportation back north. Hopefully I can reach the school before my position is given away."

And with that she gathered every ounce of courage she possessed and attempted to walk past him out the bedroom door.

She should have known she would fail. Just as she came abreast of him, he caught hold of her arm.

"You are going nowhere."

She sharply lifted her head. "I beg your pardon?"

Blast him if he wasn't grinning again and her arm wasn't tingling again. "It will be much to your benefit to stay, Miss Felicity Chambers."

"Not unless you have a wife and six children tucked away somewhere in need of instruction or a brace of girls who require deportment lessons in order to make their come-out." She was even angrier that her voice suddenly sounded so breathless. "Please let go."

He did, which surprised her. He was still blocking the door, though, which frayed her determination to get past him. There was just too much of him, and that too much seemed to throw off the most amazing heat. She thought she might be blushing again. And he'd gone very still. Even more oddly, he seemed to be staring at her as if he couldn't look away

Felicity froze, suddenly feeling like a rabbit caught in a dog's sight. Her breath seemed to seize. She couldn't move; couldn't look away from the hypnotic green of his eyes. She couldn't believe it, but he looked surprised. Maybe as surprised as she felt?

She never had the chance to ask. With one fluid movement, he cupped her face in his hands and bent to kiss her. She never even got the chance to protest or agree or even catch her breath. Suddenly she was surrounded by him; by his scent, his strength, his just-callused hands. His delicious mouth.

And it happened again. That flash of light, the shock of electricity that lit the room. A sweet, melting something that robbed her breath and set her heart pounding.

Before she could comprehend any of it, he pulled back. She blinked. Then she blinked again, caught in between breaths, her body in turmoil. What had happened? What had he done to her? Did he feel even a fraction of what she did?

Obviously not. Instead of blinking as if finding his body rearranged, he stepped away, easily letting her go. And when she stumbled a bit on suddenly shaky knees, he grinned.

"Damme if the duke doesn't have better taste than I gave him credit for," he mused, suddenly sounding quite merry.

Felicity feared she was gaping. "Pardon? The duke?"

"The very one. You are quite correct. The command came directly from him, even though in my hand. He wished you to present yourself here for my perusal. At least he was that kind about it."

Felicity feared she wasn't breathing. "Perusal?" she demanded. "For what?"

"Why to see if you'd do, of course."

Suddenly she was afraid. She took a step back and bumped into a table, making something rattle. She couldn't even find the words to challenge him. Her comprehension seemed to have disintegrated in the space of a kiss.

"Don't you want to know why?" he asked.

"For heaven's sake, Bracken," came a familiar voice from the hallway. "Just tell the girl."

Felicity almost groaned aloud. The Siren. That

was the last thing she needed, she thought in despair. The woman was more glorious than even those ankles promised. Blond, voluptuous, with deep blue eyes and a birthmark by her mouth, for heaven's sake. The sight of her managed to douse any fire Felicity might have thought she felt, leaving her quite miserable and even more confused. At least the strength flooded back into her knees.

"Tell me *what*?" she asked, already knowing she didn't want to know.

"Genève," Lord Flint objected, not smiling anymore. "You are not helping."

The siren's smile was even more glorious. Did anyone truly have such straight white teeth? Felicity mourned, instinctively running her tongue over her left canine, which slightly overlapped its neighbor.

"Well, you're not doing all that well by yourself," the beauty drawled. "Ask him again, my dear."

Felicity closed her eyes, awash in humiliation. "Very well, if it will get me out of here. What, my lord," she asked, "is this mysterious bequest?"

He chuckled. "Why, me, of course."

Felicity's eyes flew open. "I beg your pardon?"

"I am usually more fond of blonds," he admitted. "But I imagine I could learn to like brunettes quite well."

Felicity stopped breathing altogether. "For what?"

She just hoped her voice sounded as ominous as she intended.

It obviously didn't. He was smiling again, his head tilted as if assessing her reaction, his hands back on his hips. "Well, marriage, of course."

She knew she was staring, but suddenly she felt

numb and stupid. "Marriage."

He had the nerve to laugh. "You didn't think I'd want you for a mistress, did you?"

Felicity had never once fainted in her life. She didn't then. She reared back and slapped the laughing lord as hard as she could. And when he stumbled back, she stalked off, the sound of the siren's throaty laughter following her down the corridor.

CHAPTER 2

FELICITY WAS FURIOUS. SHE COULDN'T quite see well enough to get her clothing folded into her bag. She also had to keep interrupting her work to swipe at the tears that streamed down her face.

"Drat...!" She hated even more that she couldn't weep like a lady. "Blast..!" She gulped and sobbed and hiccupped. And she had no reason. She had known all along, really, that this was a mistake. That someone was making micefeet of her life for no discernible reason.

Marriage. To a duke's son. How *funny* the farce must seem to them. A true Sheridan play, right there in the family manse.

"*Damn!*"

If she could only get her cloak to fold properly, she could latch the pestilential bag and be off. Where, she wasn't certain. She wasn't even quite sure in which direction Gloucester lay. But she would find it if it killed her. Better to be found frozen in the snow than stay another minute to amuse a bored lordling and his familiar. Although, she ruefully had to admit, it would be difficult to freeze in September.

If only she understood *why*. Why her? What could she have possibly done to deserve such treatment? Who could have seen something in her that would suggest to them that she deserved to be humiliated and shamed this way? Who decided she should be the object of such a great joke?

"He didn't mean to insult you, you know."

Oh, blast. The very last thing she needed.

The Siren stood in the narrow doorway to her room like a lily at the edge of a midden. Felicity dropped her head, her hands still clutching the faded blue woolen cloak that still spilled out of her bag.

"I have no idea what the duke is thinking," the woman said in her soft, languorous voice, "but he really is intent on having you marry his son. Bracken told me all about it on the way down."

"How lovely for you. I wish someone had bothered to tell me. Or explained what the joke is."

Finally, she lifted her head, wishing she could shrill at the woman, knowing she had no reason. It wasn't the beauty's fault. She was simply trying to be kind. At least Felicity hoped she was. She didn't think she could survive another person setting her up for such a fall. And still she had to scrub the tears from her face.

"I mean no insult, Miss——-" Felicity began.

That perfect smile again. "Missus. Mrs. Genève Dent-Hardy. You are Miss Chambers?"

Instinct kicked in and pushed Felicity into a drawing room curtsy. "How do you do, Mrs. Dent-Hardy. But why has he delegated you to beard the lion in her den, as it were?"

"Oh, he doesn't know I'm here. But I couldn't allow you to leave thinking..."

Felicity's jaw came up. "Thinking what? That the nobility is so bored it must find an unprotected woman to torment? That games are more important than her livelihood or self-respect or honor?"

"But I was serious," the lordling himself piped up, stepping up next to his paramour. Before Felicity could answer, his features took on a thunderous appearance. "Is *this* where the staff put you?"

Felicity looked around the room as if she had not been shivering in it for four days. "Of course."

It was, after all, on the staff floor, a single room without fireplace or bureau or rug. It did have four hooks on the wall, though, and a tiny dormer window near the ceiling, which let in some light. Felicity had certainly occupied worse.

"Higgins!" Lord Flint suddenly bellowed, turning away from the door. "H–i–i–g–g–i–i–i–i–i–ns!!!"

Felicity looked around again. "What is wrong?"

She heard someone thundering up the narrow third-floor steps.

"My lord?" The skeletal butler appeared in the doorway, huffing and pink.

"Get Mrs. Windom up here," his employer growled. "Right. *Now!* This is inexcusable. Whose idea was it to put a guest of this house in the goddamn *attic*?!"

"My lord," the butler protested, red-faced, as he shot an uncomfortable look at Mrs. Dent-Hardy.

Thank heavens the butler hadn't been here earlier, Felicity thought. Her language would have sent him into a seizure.

"Miss Chambers is moving. *Now!*" Lord Flint

commanded. "The Chinese bedroom, do you hear me?" The young lord had his hands clenched and was leaning over the old man. "Do you *hear* me?"

"No thank you," Felicity said, finally getting her bag closed. "I would prefer Mr. Higgins get me a ride to the nearest posting house."

"Don't be absurd," Lord Flint snapped. "You'll stay here and marry me."

"Don't *you* be absurd, my lord," she said, lifting the bag in her arms. "You have no more desire to marry me than I have to marry you."

"Marry?" Higgins gasped in failing tones.

"Of course you do," Lord Flint scoffed. "No one would be idiotic enough to turn down a chance like that. You would be mistress of this house and another like it. A duke's daughter-by-marriage. A leader of fashion. Put that bag down."

Felicity bristled, back straight, chin out, cheeks hot. "My lord. Women are not afforded many choices in life. Especially poor women. Especially poor, orphaned women." Trembling with the effort, she stepped up to him, barely noticing that Mrs. Dent-Hardy scooted aside, smiling like a conspirator. She did notice that her own chin only came as high as the lordling's top jacket button. "But I do have this choice. I am going home, my lord. I am going to teach girls to maintain their self-respect as their parents auction them off like sheep in a market, and I am going to assure them that they amount to more than their piano or drawing or stitchery. Because then I can help them avoid the kind of insult I have suffered today."

And without another word, she pushed past her tormentor by the expedience of shoving her bag straight into his stomach.

"Higgins?" she asked, walking out into the hall as the lord dropped, gasping to his knees. "Do I have to walk?"

Higgins was frozen in place. "Oh, Miss…"

She sighed. "I understand. It would not be worth your job." Patting his thin arm, she stepped past. "I will not endanger another person's position."

And with annoyingly persistent tears once again streaking her cheeks, Felicity descended the stairs, never once acknowledging the sound of female hands clapping behind her except to think that Mrs. Dent-Hardy really must learn to keep her opinions to herself.

"You needn't enjoy this quite so much, Gen," Flint rasped, his stomach still sore as he straightened in time to hear the door slam three stories down.

"Oh, yes I do," she answered, patting him on the shoulder like a child. "I don't believe I have ever seen you treat a woman in so cow-handed a fashion."

He glared down the stairs, as if he could conjure the little termagant. "I have never been so provoked. What could ever make her think I was making a maygame of her?"

Gen turned a startled gaze on him. "Oh, my dear. She said she was an orphan, did she not? A poor one who managed to secure a position in a lady's academy? And you pulled her from her place of employment to leave her languishing for four days without explanation before laughingly telling her that she will marry you. What could possibly compel her to think you might not be sincere?"

Bracken closed his eyes, mortified. Furious. Resentful. Damn his father for demanding this of him.

"She might have learned if she'd stayed around."

"And she might have stayed if you had used just a bit of your legendary charm. Instead you seem to have taken out the anger that should be directed at your father on an innocent young lady."

He sighed. "I still have to figure a way to get her back here. Whether I like it or not."

Again, Genève smiled. "Well, I do believe you have met your match, my love. She will make an excellent wife."

"That termagant? I should say not. She belongs in Bedlam."

"She belongs on the throne. Don't you think, Higgins?"

Higgins was still standing like a statue at the edge of the stairs, his forehead beaded with perspiration, his eyes wide. "I think we have just suffered a close call, madame."

Gen's laugh was delighted. "Oh, how I wish I could stay and watch this play out. I suspect it will be a more delicious battle of the sexes than anything Shakespeare could come up with." Fluffing her hair a bit and straightening her signature pink roundgown, she stepped past Flint toward the stairs. "Sadly, I would be grossly *de trop* in the courting."

"Courting?" Flint snorted, rubbing at his middle. "I'd rather catch a tiger by the tail."

Still grinning, Genève offered her hand. "I suspect that will be an apt comparison."

Finally pushing himself forward, Flint held out

his elbow for her and accompanied her down the stairs, followed by the still-affronted Higgins.

"Why her?" Gen asked as they descended. "There are certainly more acceptable females out there. Do you even know who she is?"

"A classmate to my cousin Pip at that academy where she caused so much trouble."

"An orphan."

He shrugged. "Evidently."

"But attending Miss Chase's. Not exactly a workhouse."

"Not at all."

She shook her head. "You have to admit that it does sound suspect."

"The duke did not bother to over-explain himself. Simply reminded me of my promise to wed by thirty, a certain indiscretion which will not be mentioned before ladies, and gave the chit's name and direction. I suppose I should be endlessly grateful he stumbled over a candidate with all her teeth."

Although there had been that one tooth that was just a little crooked, which only served to made her look charming. Even with her face puffy and tear-stained, she was rather a pocket Venus, with thick mahogany hair, a pugnacious little jaw, and great brown eyes that snapped fire when she was angry. And that tooth he suddenly wanted to run his tongue over. Definitely not a blond, but suddenly Flint thought she would have been wasted as a blond.

What she didn't seem to be was underhanded or sly. If she had been, instead of slapping him like a villain in a melodrama, she would have stayed right here to attract his full attention. And if his father was correct, that didn't make any sense.

"And no explanation as to why you are to marry her?" Genève asked.

Flint shrugged. Oh yes, there was an explanation. Not one he could share with Gen, though. "He says all will become clear."

Gen chuckled, her voice thrumming up and down his chest. "That is what I'd be afraid of. You have to admit that even for the duke this is just a mite eccentric."

Flint rubbed at his forehead where he thought a headache might soon make an appearance. "I'll have to go after her and drag her back."

"It is that important?" she asked.

He looked around at the well-loved house with its time-darkened paneling and white linenfold walls, its family portraits and dark pastorals topped off by one rather rusty set of armor. The house had been in his grandmother's family since Queen Bess had been a girl. It had been his refuge his entire life. He knew every cranny and cherished every out-of-plumb line and eccentricity.

It was *his,* damn it. It and everything and everyone it protected. But only if the duke agreed.

Then he thought of his fiancée's tear-ravaged face. He could hate his father for this. She didn't deserve any of it.

He was bringing her back anyway.

"Vital."

And for reasons even greater than his home.

Gen took her own look around. She had spent quite a bit of time here herself, having grown up on the next estate over. "Then you are quite right.

You must run her down."

Flint sighed. He knew that. His father had given him no choice. It was the girl or the house.

If there were only a more honorable way to do this.

"I believe it's time for me to go to my own home," Gen told him as they reached the black-and-white marble entryway. "Along with everyone else. The last thing you need is an audience. And Flint?"

He stopped to attend her.

"If this plays out the way it looks, then I expect you to honor it."

He raised his eyes to hers and saw their shared history in their depths. Friends, one-time lovers, neighbors. He'd once thought she would be his wife. She'd fallen in love with somebody else, though. Her words meant that even their casual flirtation was over.

She lifted a hand to his cheek. "Make sure she understands. She will not accept a lie."

He nodded, his heart a little sore. He realized now he had held out a hope that with Gen widowed, they might find their way back together again. Depending on how things went in the next few weeks, his father had quite thoroughly put paid to that idea. Gen would never disrupt a family the way hers had been.

"I'll let you know how things fall out," he promised.

She shot him a flashing grin. "Oh, I have a feeling I'll be able to hear it from Ravenwood. I'll give Aunt Winnie a quick visit and then be gone along with the rest."

Another complication in his life. "See if she's interested in leaving anytime soon."

Gen just smiled, since both of them knew the answer to that. Aunt Winnie had been ensconced in this house as long as either of them could remember.

With one last brief kiss, Gen shooed him out the front door. "Go on. I have to breach the billiards room."

His head groom was waiting for him by the front step.

"She's gone, then," the banty Irishman said in a near-growl. "You can fire me if you want, but Billy Burke isn't one to turn away a weeping girl."

Flint thought he was doing a lot of sighing today. Good lord. She'd turned the man who'd taught him to ride against him. "You know damn well I won't fire you, Billy," he told the grizzled, bent old man. "Now go get me my curricle." "Why?" the old man demanded, hands on hips.

Flint leaned down until they were nose-to-nose. "To bring her back."

For a moment the only thing that could be heard was distant birdsong and the chuckle of the fountain on the front lawn.

Then, abruptly, Billy nodded. "Well, all right, then."

He'd spun around and was stalking over to the stables when Flint spoke up. "She rides, huh?"

The question earned him a rusty bark. "Sits like a sack o' corn."

That stopped Flint where he stood. Not at all the answer he'd expected. Billy judged everyone he met on their relationship with horseflesh.

Billy gave his head an odd shake that passed judgment and wonder. "Never sat a horse in her life, I'm guessin'. Refuses to let it stop her."

There it was then, Flint thought as he watched the bow-legged little man head for the stables. The ex-jump jockey valued bottom. Flint just wished he knew how Miss Chambers had gained the enmity of Mrs. Windom, who had exiled her to the maid's room.

But those were matters for later. Right now, he had to decide how he was going to get Miss I-Deserve-Better Chambers back.

She did, too. She had fire in her, that girl. She had more spine than many of the soldiers he'd served with. She was going to need it. At the hard crunch of gravel, Flint turned to see Billy swing the prancing chestnuts around the front drive.

"I'll be after doin' the driving," the groom informed Flint as he pulled the restive team to a halt

Flint swung up into the curricle and pushed Billy over. "You'll drive the day I'm dead. Which way did she head?"

"Jem went toward Gloucester."

Flint chucked the reins and set the horses into motion. "Then so will we."

CHAPTER 3

O NE COACHING STOP WAS PRETTY much like another. The New Inn in Gloucester was no different. A half-timbered hostelry built around a high, wide archway that opened into the courtyard and stables, it was bustling, loud, and urgent. Ostlers laughed and yelled, running passengers juggled luggage and the remains of hastily-eaten meals, and the horses stomped and shook, setting their tack to jangling in the echoing yard.

Felicity should have been nervous. After all, she was a lone woman about to climb onto the outside seat of a northbound coach with at least half a dozen strangers, three of them men who kept casting her suggestive looks. But she had not reached her age without having to face a few unpleasantries, so she tucked herself onto the bench by the inn wall, her bag wrapped safely in her arms, and watched the world go by. She had just enough money to make it back to the school. Beyond that, it didn't matter.

And then a bright blue curricle pulled by two perfectly matched chestnuts swung expertly through the archway and pulled to a precise stop right next to the stage. Felicity almost groaned out loud. There was no mistaking the bearing of the

top-hatted driver, or the anxious frown on the face
of his smaller, more grizzled companion.

She looked around. Briefly considered taking
flight. It would do no good, of course. The inn
yard was completely enclosed, with the dozen
or so people who hadn't already climbed on the
stage just as riveted by the proceedings as she was.
She had a feeling that if she tried to hide, they
would just point her out. So, she sat still, her chin
instinctively lifting, even as her hands trembled and
her skin remembered his touch.

Lord Flint tossed his reins to Billy Burke and
hopped off the vehicle, still frowning. Felicity
frowned right back.

"Where do you think you're going?" he
demanded.

She met his bright green gaze without flinching.
"Home."

"You mean back to that school. That's no home."

"It is to me." And then he surprised her all over
again. Instead of stalking up to loom his six-foot-
plus frame over her, he strolled over. Removing his
curly-brim beaver, he sat right beside her on the
bench and leaned his head back against the half-
timbered wall.

"I began this all wrong, didn't I?" he asked with a
wry smile that settled in Felicity's chest like warm
sunshine and made her hands itch to touch him,
drat him.

The fact that he laid the curly brim in his lap like
a napkin made it all the worse. "You did."

"But you're going to let me begin again."

Blast him, now she wanted to smile. "I am?"

"Of course."

"And why is that?"

"Because otherwise you will be forced to ride inside that stuffy stage for two days with enough breaks to swallow some gamy stew and share a bed with three other ladies who most certainly snore and scratch."

She refused to look at him. "Not at all."

He looked over. "Oh?"

She fought a grin. "I'm not to be on that coach. I am to be on the next. On top."

He did grin. "Even worse. Exposed to the sun, the wind, and the groping hands of that rather oily-looking rector over there. This way you can spend the next few days in the Chinese room at Hedgehog Haven...."

She was surprised into a laugh. "Hedgehog *what*?"

He pulled a face. "Are you making light of my grandmother's house?" "Your grandmother? Is she the one who named it...that?"

"Good heavens, no. She called it Glenhaven."

"I know I shall regret this. Then why Hedgehog Haven?"

His grin was piratical. "If you have to ask that question, it becomes obvious you never met my grandmother."

And suddenly she was laughing and he was grinning and she didn't want to get on that stage. "Poor old lady. To have to put up with you for a grandson."

His smile was oddly wistful. "She was a right dragon. I adored her."

Felicity felt the admission twist in her chest. "I'm sorry."

What she wanted to tell him was how much she

envied him. To have had a real grandmother. When she'd been a girl…ah, but that kind of memory was pointless, wasn't it? She didn't have a grandmother. At least not one who'd ever expressed an interest in meeting her.

Suddenly, Lord Flint held out his hand.

"Come along," he said simply. "Save me from my father's wrath."

She shook her head, even though she had a sudden overwhelming urge to wrap her fingers around that strong, graceful hand and follow him. "I will not marry you merely to prevent a tantrum. Even from a duke."

"If you had seen his tantrums, you would not be so cavalier."

"Was that his mother you named Hedgehog Haven after?"

"Yes. Her legal name was Lady Louise Ellen Margaret Flintrush Bracken. Privately we called her The Terror."

She nodded. "I imagine she cherished that."

"She did."

"Flintrush?'

He scowled. "Indeed."

She couldn't help grinning again. "Well, at least it makes a bit more sense now."

"Another of my father's ideas. He felt it would ensure that I got an estate outside the entail."

She just nodded and turned back to the busy yard.

"I agree with you," he said, sounding so blasted sincere. "It's a damnable thing. But the duke was delighted to give me an ultimatum. If I don't get to know you, I lose the house. And…."

He frowned, and suddenly Felicity was surprised to see an odd vulnerability shadow his eyes.

"…I cannot imagine living anywhere else. From the time I was ten, Gran told me that Glenhaven was my home, that I was responsible for it and its people, none other. And then proceeded to give the duke power over its future."

Damn if Felicity didn't feel sorry for him, the third son of a duke. How had that happened? How was she to escape the net he was tightening about her?

"A little odd, surely?"

He shrugged. "Gran put little reliance on men. Not surprising, really. Her own father went through two fortunes in under a decade. If her mother hadn't taken control of the finances, you would have been visiting a thatched house these past few days."

Felicity nodded. "A woman after my own heart. I wish I could have met her."

He actually shuddered. "I don't. Each of you is formidable enough on your own. Together, you might have toppled governments. Can I ask you something?"

"I don't see why not. My stage is not due for another hour."

She knew he was watching her. Still she kept her eyes on the stage as it loaded. She was already afraid if she met those lovely green eyes, she would lose her purpose. Even looking away, she swore she could feel his gaze in her chest.

"You must see you cannot leave," he said.

"I must?"

"It would be unfair to not even give me a chance

to plead my case."

She shook her head again. "If I stay in that house with you for a week, I will forfeit any respectable future."

"Even if you're chaperoned?"

Blast him. She wanted to stay. She wanted to see what might happen that could save her from a life of tending other people's children. She wanted to believe in a miraculous place where she could live in the same world as her friends from Miss Chase's. She wanted to believe, even if she knew better. It had ever been her besetting sin.

Finally, she turned to face him. "Why me?"

He gave his head a slow shake. "That I don't know. The only information I was given was that you went to school with my cousin Pip."

Those words changed everything. Felicity actually gaped. Her heart knocked into her ribs. Sitting abruptly upright, she stared hard at him. "Pip is your cousin?" she demanded.

Pip, who had championed the less fortunate among the students at their boarding school, especially orphans without a family name to protect them. Pip, who had brought whimsy and revolution to a place so grim the girls had nicknamed it Last Chance Academy. Pip, who had come from a close, extended family, a family who had often taken her in when her own parents traveled off to distant diplomatic posts.

Suddenly Felicity's heart lurched in her chest. "Sweet heavens. You're Igneous!"

He groaned. "Save me from smart women."

She couldn't seem to stop gaping. "Why didn't you tell me so in the first place?"

His scowl was playful. "You never quite gave me the chance."

She shook her head. "You should have started with that fact. I would have been much more inclined to listen. At least I wouldn't have slapped you." She paused a moment, considering. "Well. I *might* not have slapped you."

Especially considering the tales Pip shared of her older cousin who'd acted as a fond brother every time she'd been deposited in the duke's home. Frog-catching, fishing, horse racing, knightly quests shared with the boys from the next estate. Pip loved her cousin. She painted such a picture of him that the young Felicity, with no family of her own, had fallen quite in love. At least as a lonely twelve-year-old.

This wasn't the time to think of that, however. She needed to steal herself against the pull of his charm.

"I wish I could help you—" she said.

"Then do."

"I cannot."

"Cannot or will not?"

"Both. Consider. Even though Pip has spoken of you and your family, what do I really know? You are an excellent whip, you can pip a card at fifty paces, and you will put a worm on a hook for a little girl...well…at least I suppose you still would."

"I would. Would you like me to exhibit?"

She shuddered. "No, thank you."

For a moment there was silence between them. The doors slammed shut on the stage and the coachie cracked his whip, sending the horses clattering toward the street, passengers still settling themselves inside. Felicity preferred to watch that orchestrated chaos than think of the mess of her own life.

"Give me a sennight," Lord Flint suddenly said, still not moving. "Get to know Glenhaven and me. Find out if we fit you. If we don't, I will send you back in my own carriage with a note instructing the school that if they don't take you back, they will never again have the children of anyone the Duke of Lynden has ever met."

Felicity looked over at him. He looked so relaxed, lounging against the wall with his hands on his thighs and his booted feet splayed in the gravel as if her answer didn't much matter. Felicity knew better. Even if she hadn't just heard about his dilemma, she could tell by the height of his shoulders, as if he were holding himself in place, fighting against action.

She would be Pip's cousin. Pip's *family.*

Turning a bit, she then considered Billy Burke, sitting ramrod straight on the driver's perch on that sleek vehicle, the reins wrapped around his gnarled hands. He was watching her, and he was frowning. Not a 'what a horrible person' frown. A 'what will she do?' frown. He was worried for the man sitting next to her, she realized with a start, which was a change from earlier that day when he'd seen her striding into the stables, still hiccupping with tears, and he'd roundly cursed that same man.

The old man loved him, she thought. He worried for him. She ached, suddenly, for someone to worry for her. For someone who frowned for her.

She finally sighed. "I still don't understand."

Lord Flint laughed, a rueful sound. "Neither do

I. Shall we find out together?"

Blast him. She wanted to stay. She wanted to know what it would be like to have family. Her *own* family.

And yet, she knew all too well what dreams were worth.

"Stay for a week or two," he urged, "so we can talk it over without an audience."

He did have a point. In an effort to hear the conversation, the people left behind in the inn yard had stopped pretending they were occupied and just stood watching.

"You can move on, you know!" Felicity informed them all with a scowl. "Nothing is going to happen."

One farm wife laughed out loud. "Oh, no, dearie. Somethin'll happen, all right."

"But not here," Lord Flint informed the woman archly. "Because the young lady sees the wisdom of spending a vacation at a lovely estate being supervised by my Aunt, the inestimable Lady Winifred St. Clair."

"Ooooeeee," one of the grooms piped up from where he was gathering used tack. "Proper dragon, that one is, beggin' y'r pardon, my lord."

"No need," Flint said with a grin. "Unless you wish to ask it of the dragon."

The ostler brayed and slapped his knee. "Not on y'r life."

"Are there any women in your family who are *not* dragons, my lord?" Felicity asked.

"I'd say Pip, but I think all she needs is time and a good cane."

Felicity wanted so badly to smile. He was right.

Pip was impish and clever and bull-headed. Give her a proper cane, lorgnette and forty years, and she would be formidable.

"Where is she?"

"Pip? London, I think."

Felicity was the one frowning now. "Your aunt."

He grinned, and she tumbled a little harder. That dimple. "The west wing of the second floor of Glenhaven. You haven't met her?" "Not unless she was polishing brasses in the library. No."

His laugh was a bark. "In that case, she probably believes you to be another of what she calls my mad starts."

Felicity tilted her head in a perfect imitation of some of the more innocent of her pupils. "You mean like inviting a party of disreputable people to share your house with your fiancée and aunt?"

At least he had the grace to look chagrined. "They're gone now."

"I should hope so," the farm wife interjected with a disappointed shake of her head. "Otherwise I'll be taking y'r wife home with me."

"I am not his wife," Felicity objected.

"Not yet," Flint amended with a smile.

"Keep talking like that, and the word will be never."

There were grins all over the inn yard now.

"I have a note from the duke that should set her mind at ease," Lord Flint said. "The old girl is also a stickler for protocol."

Felicity actually groaned. "In that case, I sincerely doubt she'll present herself anytime soon. You cannot imagine she would recognize a girl who is unable to identify her own parents."

"If the duke told her to, she would curtsy to Napoleon. And if she recognizes you, the entire *ton* will. She might not often leave Hedgehog Haven, but she doesn't really have to. I'm surprised you haven't seen any number of visitors popping up to see her."

Still Felicity sat where she was, considering the activity in the inn yard. The entire idea was absurd. What wasn't she seeing? What question did she need to ask?

"Billy said you were interested in learning to ride," he coaxed before she could say anything. "You'd have the time to at least make a good start."

The dastard.

"Lord Flint..."

His grin was brash and bright, his eyes crinkling again. "The name is Flint. Or Bracken if you feel peevish."

"I never feel peevish," she assured him with a sniff. "Although if I were to succumb, I have a feeling you would be the instigation."

"Well, come along and find out."

Felicity just stared at him.

"Make up y'r mind, dearie," the farm wife demanded. "We got a stage to catch."

"Oh, for the love of heaven," Felicity snapped, jumping to her feet. "Fine. I'll go."

Swinging around, she leveled a glare on her companion that should have frozen his eyes. He lifted his hands in a gesture of innocence and almost popped himself in the eye with his hat. Giving him one last glare, Felicity shoved the bag into his arms, straightened her skirts, and marched over to the curricle.

"Well?" she demanded of the diminutive head groom who was grinning at her from the driver's seat.

Billy Burke jumped right down and held his hand out, his bright blue eyes twinkling. "Ah, sure now, he's not all that bad. He can ride like the devil, and you saw him wield these horses here, all right."

Felicity chuckled. "Indeed. What else do I need to know?"

Without another objection, she let the little man hand her up onto the coach. After all, he did have a point. Besides, the stables at Glenhaven did have some fine horseflesh in them, which had been the only thing keeping Felicity at the house even this long. The least the Bracken family could do for her was give her a few more days in the saddle.

Tossing the carpetbag up, Lord Flint climbed into his own seat with a grumble and gathered the reins in his gloved hands as Billy Burke took up his perch behind. Waiting only until the curricle creaked with the little man's weight, Bracken flipped the reins and turned the restive chestnuts back through the gates.

Felicity didn't realize how glad she was to go until she heard clapping from their audience back in the yard. "I wouldn'ta told him no neither," she heard from the farmwife as they passed through the archway onto the high street.

It was obvious Lord Flint had heard it, too by the grin on his face.

For not the first time, Felicity wondered if she were making a mistake.

CHAPTER 4

A S HE GUIDED THE SLEEK curricle through the Gloucester traffic, Flint fought a surge of ambivalence. He had succeeded in getting Felicity off the coach. But as he swerved around a beer wagon, he saw the tall squared-off bell tower of Gloucester Cathedral lurking over the rooftops, as if judgment were following him through the streets. The results of his actions would be good for him. But would they be good for Felicity Chambers?

Assuredly not. And there was nothing he could do about it.

"Felicity...." he began.

"Miss Chambers," she immediately corrected like the veriest deb.

He fought a fresh grin. She kept surprising him, although he wasn't sure why. If she had survived that awful school she'd been condemned to, especially as an orphan, she had to have her share of grit.

Pip had filled him in on the draconian conditions that had existed until his spitfire of a cousin had fomented rebellion. The girls had been sent for their safety to the most unsafe place in Britain. And Felicity would have been caught dead center without even the protection of a family. It once again occurred to Flint to wonder why.

"*Miss* Chambers," he corrected, knowing damn well Billy Burke had a big grin on his face where he was perched up behind. "How about we put a two-week deadline on our little mission?"

"*Your* mission," she corrected, eyes straight ahead, hands clasped in her lap.

He wanted to smile again. Most people new to his driving would have been clutching the railing like a drowning person. Felicity seemed perfectly comfortable swaying with the motion as if she were seated on a ship in high water. He was impressed.

"Well," he said, his own attention back on Mack and Jack as the horses threw up their heads at an urchin who chose that moment to dart into the street.

"Here now, lads," he calmed them, pulling them out of the way.

The child skidded to a stop and shot Flint a cheeky grin and a tip of his disreputable cap. The horses snorted at the boy as if he had earned their disgust. Alongside him Flint heard a breathy little chortle and felt a bit better. At least she wasn't weeping.

"As I was saying," he said, easing the reins a bit as they reached the edge of town to give the horses their heads. He didn't like it that he still hadn't escaped the shadow of that bloody bell tower. Did everyone in this town feel judged, as if God were glowering down at them?

"As you were saying," Felicity prompted.

"Yes. As I was saying. We both have a mission. Mine is to try to talk you into marrying me..."

"Because of your high regard for me."

He chuckled. "Keep showing me such sass, and I will have a very high regard for you. You should know Pip is my favorite cousin, and you remind me of her a bit."

Next to him, Felicity seemed to slump a bit.

"She is well?" she asked, sounding more tentative than she had since he'd met her. "I haven't been able to...well..."

He shot her a quick look to see the sadness in her rich brown eyes. "Difficult for a teacher in a young ladies' academy to mingle with the *ton*?"

She shrugged. "Pip would have it otherwise, but you know Pip."

He smiled again. "Pip invited Brady the gardener to her come-out ball. She even danced with him, much to the chagrin of both her mother and my mother."

Finally, he got a smile out of her, and it was a beauty, sparkling and sharp.

"She considers Brady to be more of a good influence than most of her family."

"Probably for good reason. We're a rather reprehensible lot."

There was a brief, sudden silence. "Probably not the way you want to convince a girl to marry you."

He shrugged. "You've known all along what kind of family we are. It's not exactly a surprise."

"True." She sighed. "Why, then, should I trust you enough to put my future into your hands?"

"*Why*? Because I am a nonpareil, of course."

"An excellent thing to be if I were a horse."

"Top of the trees."

"Botany bores me."

"Well-breeched."

"Only if you marry me."

It was his turn to sigh. "True."

Not true. What he had to do was far worse.

And then she had to go and smile, a small, sly quirk to her lips he almost missed. She should have been quite forgettable, a tiny thing with a rather plump figure and freckles sprinkled across her nose. And yet there was something devilishly attractive about those soft brown eyes.

They rode on in silence until the gates to Glenhaven appeared. Easily swinging the horses through, Flint followed the familiar lane. It wasn't an opulent property. He would have called it a tidy inheritance, with quite enough profit to keep him comfortable when paired with his inheritance from his mother's mother. He had always considered it his own promised haven, mostly safe from his father's interference. For some reason, he wanted Felicity to like it.

New guests were greeted by lion-topped stone gate posts, the gatehouse now empty where it looked over a long avenue of beeches, whose yellowing leaves rustled in the afternoon breeze. A herd of fallow dear could be seen in the distance cropping the back lawn.

"What is that?" Felicity asked, pointing to the round white building perched on the edge of an ornamental pond. "A Greek temple? Isn't that a bit pretentious?" "It was my grandmother's favorite place to spend an afternoon," he said. "She said it held memories."

They had found her there, that last day, curled up on the sofa, a book on her lap and an early rose in her hand. Ninety-two, and she'd walked half a mile to be in that gazebo for her last breath.

"I'm sorry," Felicity said. "Pip said you were very close."

Flint nodded. "We were."

It was the house itself, though, that held Flint's best memories. Ah, there it was, just appearing around the last corner, a pink brick E from that lady's reign, with row upon row of sparkling windows and a forest of chimneys littering the roof like a copse of trees. The front door was heavy carved oak and crowned by a triangular pediment bearing the griffon of the Flintrush crest.

It was nothing fancy, in fact a burr under his father's saddle. A duke demanded more regal rooms, a more intimidating façade, he kept insisting. The duke had pestered his mother for years to tear the old girl down and replace it with Palladio's best. The only woman in the world the duke had not been able to intimidate had simply stared him down until passing the antique gem off to the only other person who felt compelled to keep it intact.

With stipulations, of course.

Flint wasn't sure whether it was a punishment for her grandson's lack of purpose in life, or her son's arrogance. Her son might have been a duke, but his mother had been a chandler's granddaughter. And she never wanted him to forget it.

A sigh from Felicity brought Flint back to himself just in time to avoid driving into the ornamental pond.

"I can't say I would not have made the same decision," she admitted, head up to take in the comfortable lines of the house. "If it were mine."

He took a quick look over to catch a wistful expression in her eyes. Damn, but he wanted her to like the place, no matter that it might not help either of them.

He pulled the horses to a stop in front of the door. "It could be."

She shook her head. "No, it cannot. No woman owns her own house. She doesn't own anything. She lives in a man's house at his pleasure, and when he dies, at his son's."

He found himself blinking. "Her son's, too."

She stretched her head back to take in the façade. "Indeed. Her son who will marry and evict his mother to the dower house so another woman may temporarily live under his roof."

For a moment, Flint just sat there staring at this mouse of a woman with her soft eyes and thick brown hair and razor-sharp tongue. She was right, of course. He'd never really thought of it that way, probably because his grandmother had somehow blackmailed her own son into leaving her alone in the one place she most wanted to be.

"I would leave it to you if I could," he said.

She smiled, and again he noticed how it changed her features, as if it suddenly made her visible. "No, you wouldn't. You would leave it to your son, just as generations have before. I did not say I don't understand the laws of primogeniture. I said I wish there was room for women in there somewhere."

And without another word or assistance, she climbed down off the curricle.

Evidently Flint preferred to get over rough

ground quickly. Felicity had barely had the chance to hand her bonnet and cloak off to Higgins before Flint had her by the hand and was dragging her up the grand staircase.

"Have Mrs. Windom in my office in fifteen minutes, Higgins," he said as he led the way.

Poor Higgins looked as if he'd rather eat nails. Even so, he dropped a pro forma bow and headed in the other direction.

"You won't like Aunt Winnie," Flint was saying. "Nobody does. But she's absolutely necessary for your reputation."

"If no one likes her, why do so many visit?"

"Because she is the highest *ton*. Only person in society who makes Mrs. Drummond–Burrell quake in her shoes."

Felicity shook her head, her equanimity leaking away like milk through a sieve. "She is your aunt? On whose side?"

"My mother's." It seemed he had to think about that. "More of a cousin, actually. But only she and Mother seem to be able to work out the connection."

"Was she your grandmother's companion?"

He gave a short bark of laughter. "Gad, no. The two of them were like lionesses marking territory. I'm not sure if they had been friends or she just blackmailed Gran into letting her stay."

They reached the first floor and turned for the next set of steps, all of them lined with dark portraits of people in ruffs.

"A poor relation?"

"Rich as Croesus."

So, Felicity thought, *a nasty old woman with money*

living off her relatives. We ought to get along famously.
She almost sighed out loud. It was becoming clear
that she should have taken that stage.

The hallway they progressed down was one
Felicity hadn't had a chance to investigate, just
beyond the family hall where Flint's room lay.
Probably for the better. She couldn't imagine how
difficult her stay would have been if she'd shoved
open a door to find the old lady at her bath.

Flint rapped sharply on a door towards the
end of the hall. "My room is at the other end of
the corridor," he said, then grinned. "If you feel
compelled to visit."

"I know." She refused to let him see what his
casual flirtation did to her breathing. "And no. I've
done my visiting."

The door before them was opened by a tall,
elegant, middle-aged blond lady in sensible gray
serge. Seeing Flint, she smiled and curtsied. "My
lord."

"Does he have his tart with him?" a warbling
voice demanded from farther inside the apartment.

"No!" Felicity called back before anyone had a
chance to stop her. "I am the decent one!"

Astonishingly, she earned a rusty laugh. "Then
get in here and let me have a look at you!"

This was evidently not Aunt Winnie's customary
greeting, if judged by the astonished look on not
only Flint's face, but the lovely blond lady.

"Miss Mary Fare," Flint said, ignoring his cousin
as he dropped a bow to the woman who had met
them. "May I present my fiancée, Miss Chambers?"

"Not his fiancée," Felicity corrected, dropping
her own curtsy.

Miss Fare matched it perfectly and shred a genuine smile.

"Felicity," Flint said. "Miss Fare is my aunt's companion. She is all that keeps us from mayhem."

Miss Fare answered with a gentle smile. "This is the most excitement we've had here since the hunting party."

Flint grimaced. "If you love me, do not bring up the hunting party."

Felicity lifted an eyebrow. "Oh, no, I think Miss Fare must tell me all about it."

"What are you all waiting on," Aunt Winnie demanded with a *thud* Felicity recognized as a cane hitting the ground, "a master of ceremonies?"

Laying a hand against the small of Felicity's back, Flint ushered her in. Felicity would have been far happier if she hadn't felt that odd sparking again. It distracted her at a moment when she thought she needed all her wits about her.

She stepped into the parlor and knew she was right. The room was over-warm and stuffed with an astonishing amount of furniture, as if the old woman had decided to empty out an entire house into these two rooms. Two tall, carved wooden chairs bracketed the roaring fireplace. Seated on one, her feet resting on a tapestried ottoman, was the tiniest woman Felicity had ever seen. It was rare that Felicity actually felt tall. She did now as she approached the wrinkled, beringed doyen.

But it wasn't height or embellishment or the morning dress that looked as if it had been constructed from red brocade bed curtains that really caught Felicity's attention. It was the lady's hair. It was purple. Not a soft lavender, or lilac, although even those would have been noteworthy. This hair was bright, curling purple.

Felicity caught herself just shy of bursting into laughter. If this was to be her reputation, she was doomed. Who could take this little elf seriously?

And then Felicity looked into those large black eyes and curtsied before she even realized it. "Madame," she greeted the old woman.

"Miss Winifred St. Clair," Lord Flint intoned with his own courtly bow. "Allow me to present to you, Miss Felicity Chamber."

"*Hmmph.*" The bright eyes swung over to take in Flint. "Your father sent me a message," she barked.

Felicity had been right. The little woman did have a cane, a gold-topped hickory affair she slammed into the floor once again. And not onto the carpet. Onto the bare wood, so that the *crack* echoed. "Is this the chit I'm to give countenance to?"

Flint smiled. "It is."

"*Hmmph.*" She yanked a gold lorgnette from her lap and took a leisurely perusal. Having suffered her share of perusals over the years, Felicity stood still.

"Shall I turn about so you can see the aft end?" she asked. "Or open my mouth wide enough for you to check my teeth?"

The woman's scowl was magnificent. "Well, you're the saucy one, aren't you? What makes you think you can be so full of brass?"

Felicity shrugged. "I have undoubtedly already lost my teaching position. I have been told I am to marry a perfect stranger for no good reason I can see, and was foolish enough to agree to two weeks in which he might try to convince me. I have nowhere to go, no one to see. I imagine I have little to lose."

"How tall are you?" "Five-foot one inch."

She snorted. "Well, there's that. Don't have to stand on a stool to talk to ya."

"Indeed. I imagine that gets old when living in the same house as his lordship."

The old lady waved the lorgnette. "What, him? The devil with it. I never see him. The only time he's here is with his disreputable friends, and he's too afraid to let me loose on them to introduce me." Her face folded into a thousand wrinkles. "Even though I know most of them anyway."

Felicity looked over to see that Flint was singularly undismayed by the statement.

"You terrify them," he assured the old woman. "And if one is to throw a hunting party, you hope the only one terrified is the fox."

The old woman maintained her glare. Flint grinned back.

"She won't do," she snapped, swinging the cane so swiftly at Felicity, she had to stumble back rather than get rapped on the jaw. "Not at all."

Flint shrugged. "Tell His Grace. It was his idea."

"Why?"

"We have just been having that discussion," Felicity said. "I assume this means that you don't know either?"

"I do not. And I refuse to countenance what I don't understand. What if one of my friends stops by and sees her? It is unconscionable."

"She went to school with Pip," Flint said, pulling out a snuff box and flipping the lid open.

"So did forty other gels. And all of them have

surnames."

Flint's one eyebrow headed north; his actions momentarily paused.

"I have a surname," Felicity assured her. "I made it up myself."

That really earned her a glare. "You have no idea who your people are?"

"Not a one. I was told I was left at a private home in the country for my first five years. The only thing I remember from that time was two other small children and a goat who was forever stealing my biscuits."

"So then, you come from people with means."

It was Felicity's turn to shrug. "So we have always assumed. I never wanted for anything." Except affection, history, people to call her own.

"And then?"

"I was sent to Last...er...Lady Chase's Academy for Young Ladies, where I stayed until I graduated three years ago and went to my first position."

Again they waited, all standing around that Gothic old chair like supplicants before a bishop. Felicity couldn't understand how Flint could look so cool and unconcerned. She was beginning to feel limp and wet from the unbearable heat in this cramped little room. She didn't even want to consider it might also have been from tension. Did she want this old woman to accept her? *Did* she want to stay?

She was standing at attention, hands clasped in front of her as if awaiting punishment. As for Flint, he was languidly dabbing snuff onto the hollow between his thumb and forefinger and taking a sniff.

Felicity looked closer. She might be mad, but she could swear that he inhaled nothing. She afforded him a brief, sly glance to see him pulling out his handkerchief to brush at his suit coat, an aristocratic gentleman at his most officious. Which suddenly seemed odd.

She never had the chance to challenge him. Suddenly his aunt, or cousin, or whatever she was, straightened in her seat and gave a resounding thump of her cane.

"You might as well go back to where you came from," she pronounced down her hawklike nose. "I refuse to countenance you."

And Felicity, who had abruptly gotten her wish, was surprised by a sting of tears.

"Excellent," she answered, straightening as if it didn't matter. "Then I can be on my way."

Although where, inevitably, she had no idea. Perhaps the school would be considerate. In any case, it was well past time for her to go.

CHAPTER 5

"RUDE MISS!" MISS ST. CLAIRE snapped. Felicity didn't bother to turn around. She needed to get out of the room before either that nasty old woman or her companion saw the sheen in her eyes.

"One moment please, Miss Chambers," Lord Flint said, never raising his voice. "Higgins."

Higgins stepped right into Felicity's path and bowed. She let him by.

"My lord?" he asked.

"Instruct Mrs. Windom to begin organizing Miss St. Clair's removal." Felicity stuttered to a halt and spun about. Higgins gaped. Miss Fare paled.

Lord Flint seemed to notice none of that. He was locked in silent combat with his aunt. "It is His Grace's wish that if Miss St. Clair cannot see her way to assist Miss Felicity, that she is welcome to return to her own home."

Felicity couldn't look away from that frigid contest. Flint stood completely still, looking as relaxed as if he were making a morning call. His aunt all but vibrated with fury, her fingers taut as claws on the carved arms of the chair.

"You wouldn't," the old woman rasped.

Was Felicity the only one who saw that terrible fear flare in those sharp old eyes? The vulnerability? Within the space of a few words, she looked suddenly old.

Flint shrugged. "It is not my decision, ma'am. It is my father's."

Felicity felt a hot rage ignite in her. Why torture that poor woman? No matter the visitors, that one glance of stark terror betrayed that she was old and alone except for the place she held in this house. And Felicity didn't want any other person to know what it was like to be abandoned, no matter how surly they were, or how much they deserved it.

She swung around on Flint. "How dare you?" she demanded.

She wasn't certain who was more astonished, Flint or his aunt. They both gaped at her as if she were a talking dog.

"Pardon?" Flint asked.

Felicity advanced on him. "A gentleman does not extort a frail old woman to go against her moral code. Your cousin does not feel able to support a bastard. I understand that."

Felicity heard gasps. Even Flint looked uncomfortable.

She focused on him, the cause of her distress. "Why be delicate about this?" she demanded. "It is obvious what I am. I have lived with the truth my whole life. I have also spent a lifetime being met with just such disgust, so do not think I shall shrivel and die. Your cousin has just learned that she is expected to accept that which to her is unacceptable. And yet you expect her to throw over decades of training and perjure herself about how delighted she will be to welcome me into her home."

"*My* home," he said, his voice still perfectly calm.

Felicity snorted. "It will be your home when you actually inhabit it. There is not a thing in this house that tells me you have ever so much as set foot inside. It could belong to anyone. This," she said, swinging her arms wide to include the cluttered rooms, "belongs to someone. It belongs to your aunt. So, she is the one with the right to accept or reject me here. She has rejected me. If you do not wish to lend me conveyance into Gloucester, I will simply walk. I know which way to go now."

Well, she thought she did.

She turned again to go, trying so hard not to let Miss Fare see the new tears that threatened. Instead Higgins saw them.

"Higgins..." she began.

"It would be my honor," he said with a formal bow. "If that is what you wish."

"I am *not* frail," Felicity heard behind her and almost smiled.

"Higgins," Flint said, "if you let her walk out of this house, you go right after her."

"Yes, my lord." Higgins dropped a precise bow to the room and turned to follow Felicity.

She heard Flint sigh.

"Please," he said, sounding wry. "Stay a bit longer, Miss Chambers."

Felicity halted in the hallway. "Please?" she echoed, careful not to let anyone see her relief.

"Hadn't I said that?"

She shook her head. Higgins shook his head. Miss Fare shook her head.

"No," they all said in unison.

Felicity finally turned to see the rueful grin on Flint's face.

"My sincere apologies, Miss Chambers," he said with a bow that rivaled Higgins's. "I must have gotten ahead of myself. Will you stay while we sort this out?"

"As long as tossing your aunt out into the snow is not part of that sorting."

He was now fighting a grin. "Difficult to do in September."

There was another resounding *thunk* of the cane hitting the floor. "His *frail* aunt is right over here."

No one moved for what seemed like an eternity.

"What room have you given her?" Miss St. Clair demanded.

"She will be given the Chinese bedroom," Flint said.

The old woman nodded. "About time. That old besom you have in charge exiled her up in the maid's wing."

"Yes, we'll be discussing that as soon as I finish here."

"You going to dismiss her?"

"Mrs. Windom? Should I?"

Felicity got another quick look from the old woman. "No. Let this one do it when she's in charge."

Finally, Felicity made a move. "Oh, no..."

"Oh, yes," the old woman retorted. "If you mean to be in this family, you need to learn how to deal with the servants."

"But I don't mean to be in this family."

"Too late." She waved a gnarled old hand. "Now

be off. You have worn me out."

"Then I may assume poor Higgins doesn't have to be hauling all this Gothic nonsense down the stairs?" Flint asked.

She huffed, sounding stronger by the minute. "As if he would. Higgins knows who's in charge here."

"Until I make Miss Chambers my wife."

"And Miss Chambers is right *here,*" Felicity snapped.

"Indeed you are," Flint said, and held out his elbow for her. "Shall we make a dignified retreat?"

She laid her fingers on his arm. "Might as well."

They nodded to Miss Fare and stepped into the hallway. Higgins closed the door behind them and followed at a safe distance. "You didn't seem unduly upset by your aunt's behavior," Felicity said as she walked.

Flint shrugged. "Something like this happens every time I'm here."

"If you'll pardon my saying so, sir," Higgins said from where he brought up the rear, "the threat from His Grace was new."

Flint smiled. "Yes. Well, don't tell His Grace. There's a good man."

This time Felicity swore it was Higgins who snorted.

Mrs. Windom sat in the back parlor as if she were in the dock before a judge. A thin, precise woman, she was perched on a hard-back chair with her feet planted in perfect parallels and her hands clasped in her black-serge-clad lap, her unremarkable face rigidly bland, albeit pale. Felicity all but sighed out loud. She recognized this expression as well. Confusion, terror, the look of a woman who had set a foot on firm ground and felt it sink beneath her.

"If you wish me to stay in this house," Felicity told Flint beneath her breath, "you will let me handle this."

She got the kind of glare that had been bred into generations of ducal offspring. It was easy enough to recognize after spending a childhood schooling alongside their daughters and working for more of their ilk. She answered it with a calm silence, the kind governesses use with recalcitrant heirs.

He huffed. He actually huffed. Felicity took it as assent and turned to the too-still housekeeper whose hands were clenched so tightly in her lap her knuckles had blanched.

"Did Lord Flint instruct you about which bedroom to appoint for me?" Felicity asked gently.

Flint glared again. Mrs. Windom, surprisingly, hiccupped. "N...no, Miss. We were given no instructions except keep you here 'til he arrived."

Felicity let go of Flint's arm and slipped into a violet-hued armless chair across from the matching one the housekeeper occupied. "What was I wearing when I arrived?"

Mrs. Windom frowned, obviously expecting a trap. "What you're wearing now, Miss."

Felicity nodded. "Lord Flint? What am I wearing now?"

He didn't hesitate. "A shapeless brown sack that looks like you stole it straight off a horse's nose."

"And have you ever seen anyone dressed like this installed in the Chinese bedroom?"

He had the grace not to answer at all.

"What did you think when I arrived, Mrs. Windom?" Felicity asked. "In my shapeless sack with one very battered portmanteau and hard-soled working shoes?"

Because only the child of a ducal family would think that any housekeeper worth her salt would place someone who looked worse than any of her underlings into a family or guest room. Felicity just wanted Lord Flint to understand.

But Mrs. Windom didn't give the answer Felicity expected, that she had thought Felicity to be a new housemaid or a nanny awaiting visitors.

"Well, Miss, I thought you was the same as the other women." Mrs. Windom still looked bemused. "And we always put them upstairs."

Felicity blinked, sure she'd heard wrong. "What?" she demanded, turning to glare at Flint.

But he was staring at Mrs. Windom as if she'd grown fins. "*What?!*"

Mrs. Windom blinked and hiccupped. "Pardon, my lord. I hiccup when my nerves...."

He waved her off. "Just tell me. What women you're always putting upstairs?"

"You mean you don't know?" Felicity asked.

"Of course, I don't know! Does my aunt know?" he asked Mrs. Windom.

"Of course not!" the housekeeper retorted, then hiccupped again. "We were instructed not to inform her."

"Women," he said, his frown terrifying. "How long has this been going on?"

The housekeeper pressed her fingers over her lips after another unseemly noise. "But...they've always come," she said. "Since right after your lady grandmother..."

"*Always?*" Flint demanded. "But who sends them?"

She frowned. "You mean you don't?"

For the first time in days, Felicity thought she might actually enjoy herself.

"If you could, Mrs. Windom," she said. "Tell us how they come. Who contacts you. How long they stay. Where they go."

"Well, I don't know," Mrs. Windom protested, "do I?"

"What," Flint asked in deadly tones, "*do* you know?"

He only succeeded in setting off more hiccups.

"Sit down, my lord," Felicity suggested.

"What?"

"You loom, sir. Please. Sit down before the woman has a spasm."

He sat with very little patience. "I apologize, Mrs. Windom," he said. "But I have no idea about any women. Which means someone else is using my house without either my knowledge or permission. You truly thought that...*I*...sent them?"

His housekeeper nodded, gave one more hiccup and looked to Felicity. "Of course. It's Mr. Burke brings 'em here, after all. And he always has a note from your Mr. Everhill. To hold the ladies here until they're collected."

"*Collected?*" Felicity demanded, turning to Flint.

But he was already back on his feet. "Hi-i-i-g-g-i-i-i-i-n-s!"

Felicity rubbed at the headache that had begun to bloom with all the bellowing. "You really must stop doing that."

"H–i–i–i–g–g–i–i–i–i–i–n–s!!"

Inevitably, footsteps thundered down the hallway in their direction. No wonder Higgins had maintained his youthful figure, Felicity thought inconsequentially. He was always moving faster than an army at double-march.

"My lord," he greeted them as he skidded to a stop in the doorway.

"Do you know anything about a series of women who have been making free with my staff bedrooms these last two years?"

Tugging his jacket straight, Higgins blinked as if caught in a bright light. "But of course, my lord."

Now his employer was rubbing the side of his head. "How many?"

"Well..." The dignified man cast a questioning look at Mrs. Windom. "Twelve, perhaps?"

"Twelve. Women." Flint was shaking his head. "Young? Old? Pretty? Rich? Poor?"

"Er...working class? Young all. Rather...thin, many. Quiet."

"Did you think I was another?" Felicity asked.

Higgins blinked again. "Excuse me, Miss. You aren't?" "I don't believe so, Higgins. Unless the others were expected to marry the master as well."

He just gave a mute shake of the head.

"Then why were they here?" Flint demanded, his voice rising.

He earned no more than another mute shake of the head.

"Well, why don't you know?" he all but yelled.

That, finally, made Felicity laugh. "Because it wasn't their job to know, you great lummox."

Flint spun on her. "Surely they had ideas."

"Not if they wished to maintain their places. Please, Higgins," she said, facing the now–also–pale butler. "Have a seat."

"No," Flint snapped. "Send for Burke. Tell him he'd better be here within five minutes or just keep walking down the lane."

Higgins fled.

"You'd make a terrible housekeeper," Felicity muttered, eyes closed.

She was surprised by Flint's outraged huff. "Why?"

Her eyes still closed, she smiled. "Because if your silver began to go missing, no one would tell you where."

"And you could do better?"

"As I have acted as housekeeper in a pinch, yes."

"Fine. Question Burke, then. I'm sure you two get along well enough he'd spill any secrets in your shell–like ear."

Felicity's eyes popped open. *Shell-like?*

"Is there anything you can add, Mrs. Windom?" she asked, deliberately turning away from such a slip. "Do the women have particular accents, or share any personal information? Did you think anything nefarious was going on?"

Mrs. Windom straightened like the face of Judgment. "Not in *my* house there wasn't." She spared a glare at her employer. "But once they left here, how can I know? I fed 'em up until they got pink in their cheeks and sewed new dresses myself to replace the rags they came in, and sent 'em on their way with a basket when their time came." She blushed heartily. "I was sewing one for you,

Miss."

For the first time in far too long, Felicity felt the sharp light of kindness warm her. "Thank you, Mrs. Windom. I cannot tell you what that means to me. Save it for the next."

"There will be no *next*," Flint assured them, retaking his seat.

"Accents were all different," Mrs. Windom mused. "Some from London, some north, some... well, foreign-like. Not Frenchies, but not good English. Young. Skittish as new foals near a dog, if you'll pardon my saying so."

"And none of them told you anything of where they'd been," Flint asked more gently now. "Where they were supposed to go?"

Mrs. Windom shook her head. "Mostly no more'n please and thank you. Hello, goodbye. Stayed in their room."

Flint was rubbing his head again. Felicity actually felt for him. She couldn't imagine him liking a surprise like this.

"And my aunt never knew?" Flint asked. "And wouldn't the old besom have told the world, now?" Billy Burke suddenly spoke up from the doorway.

Everyone turned his way. He stood just outside in the hallway in muddy boots and broadcloth, his hat still in his hand, Higgins waiting behind him. Felicity didn't blame the butler. She would have wanted to hear the rest as well.

"She had visitors in here every week, all right. It was hard enough keepin' 'em on her side of the house so's the young ladies would be protected."

"I assume you're about to explain, Burke," Flint said in a lazy drawl that didn't fool anybody. Even

Felicity tensed.

And then she saw the real hurt flare in Flint's eyes as he faced the man who had put him on his first horse.

"And didn't he think you wouldn't be around enough to notice, then?" the banty Irishman said, just as calmly.

"Who?" Flint asked. "Who has been using my home, as if I didn't know?" He pulled out his snuff box and flipped it open. "And while you're at it, you might as well tell me why."

Felicity noticed that he didn't offer to let Burke sit or rest anywhere. Burke didn't seem to notice.

"Your father, o' course," he said. "The duke."

"Why?"

Burke gave an eloquent shrug. "Dukes don't share their thoughts with the likes of me, sir, now, do they?"

Flint took a pinch of snuff, inhaled, and pulled out his kerchief to brush loose flakes. "And you just carted young women around for the duke without asking his purpose?"

"Not past makin' sure no harm was comin' to 'em, like. Put each of 'em on a Bristol ship for America with a packet of papers from Mr. Everhill."

"My estate manager."

"The same."

Flint nodded absently. "And you picked them up?"

"Three Tuns on the London Road. All waiting in the first bedroom. With a maid."

Which meant, Felicity was relieved to know, that they had not been taken advantage of.

Flint was still nodding, his attention on the

small gold snuffbox he flipped about in his left palm. "I imagine Mr. Everhill is not nearby to be questioned."

"In London," Burke said. "Duke was after wantin' him."

Lord Flint nodded absently, still focused on the snuff box in his hand, the top glinting gold as he turned it.

"If I find any of my staff has gone behind my back again, no matter who instructs them, they will be summarily fired without reference. Am I clear?"

Burke didn't move. Mrs. Windom and Higgins nodded.

"There will be no more women lodged in the servants' quarters who do not draw their pay from this house unless I am the one to tell you so. I will so notify the duke."

There was another round of nods.

"One thing, my lord," Burke quietly said, not moving.

Flint looked up, and Felicity was glad he wasn't angry at her.

"Yes, Burke?"

Burke motioned upward. "What do I do with the one I just brought?"

CHAPTER 6

"LORD FLINT...LORD...*FLINT!*" FELICITY GASPED AS she hurried up the stairs after him, Burke following her and Mrs. Windom following him.

"Don't you scare that poor girl," the housekeeper panted on a hiccup.

Lord Flint stopped so quickly Felicity almost caromed off him. "I have no intention of scaring her," he said, glaring back at them all. "I just want answers."

"Once you revive her from the swoon she'll fall into the minute you burst into her room like the Furies," Felicity retorted.

He glared. "The Furies were women."

She glared right back. "I doubt your guest will notice the difference."

He returned her glare, hand on the banister. "I'm quite certain you have a better idea."

"Than terrifying her after she's just arrived from who knows where?" "The Three Tuns."

Felicity scowled. "You know what I mean. If none of the women has broken their silence yet, chances are they have been forbidden to speak," she said, head back to keep eye contact with her alleged fiancé. "And I doubt a frontal attack will make a difference."

Lord Flint sighed. "It does occur to me, Miss Chambers," he said, looking none too pleased, "that for a woman who was only last week a junior teacher of penmanship and shower baths—"

"Piano and deportment."

"—you manage to be far more assertive than one would anticipate."

She flashed him a grin. "Blame Pip. She brought me out of my shell."

He groaned. "I'm sorry I didn't meet you before she did. You might have been more manageable."

Felicity saw the spark of humor in his eyes and chuckled. Blast him. She was truly enjoying sparring with him. It fizzed in her chest like a stolen sip of champagne and made her want more.

"Pip would want me to tell you that you wouldn't have liked me like that."

He shook his head and smiled. "Yes, Pip would. Now then, what exactly did you have to say about Miss—-" He looked down at Mrs. Windom.

"Murphy," the woman said with a definite nod.

"Miss Murphy." He nodded. "Irish, then."

"Not so you'd notice," Mrs. Windom said.

"Gently," Felicity said. "That's all. Go gently with her."

He huffed again. "You make it sound as if I plan to flog her."

Then without another word, he turned back up the narrow stairs to the maids' wing. "The staff is elsewhere, Mrs. Windom?"

"At dinner, my lord."

He nodded.

Reaching the third floor, he knocked on the first door on the right. For a moment there was only silence. Felicity found herself holding her breath, although she didn't know why.

Then the door eased open to reveal the newest houseguest. Mrs. Windom hadn't exaggerated. The girl might have been Felicity's age or a bit older, and she was tall, far taller than Felicity, and almost gaunt, her faded blue roundgown all but hanging off her. Her hair, scraped ruthlessly back into a bun, was a thin, watery blond, and her features would probably end up being round and pretty with a bit of weight on her.

She had beautiful blue eyes, though. Instead of lowering them as was the norm, she kept them fixed on Lord Flint, wide and staring, a rabbit keeping sight of the fox.

"Miss Murphy?" Lord Flint greeted her, his voice gentler than it had ever been with Felicity, which made her relax a bit.

Then he smiled, and even Miss Murphy relaxed a bit.

"This is the master, Nora," Mrs. Windom said. "It's his house you're in."

Miss Murphy bobbed a curtsy.

"May we speak to you a moment?" Lord Flint asked.

The girl looked over her shoulder into the narrow, bare room. "Er...I..."

"Well, that was maladroit of me, wasn't it?" He looked down at his own staff as if waiting for an idea or chairs, whichever came first.

Felicity shook her head, even more amused. "The Chinese Suite has a lovely little sitting room," she offered. "Maybe we could go there."

Flint blinked at her. "How do you know? You haven't moved yet."

She grinned at him. "There was very little to do the last four days."

So, they retreated to the Chinese Suite a floor below; Lord Flint and Felicity, anyway. Higgins and Mrs. Windom, not voluntarily, were sent for refreshments.

"Now then," Flint said, flipping his tails and taking one of the red silk chairs.

Felicity sat on the gold settee. Miss Murphy stood very straight and still next to her until Lord Flint remembered to motion her down into another red silk chair.

"You were brought here by my coachman," Flint began.

Miss Murphy cast a quick look around, as if expecting eavesdroppers. "I was, my lord."

"Can you tell me from where?"

"The Three Tuns."

Flint nodded. "Before that."

The girl sat mute. Flint waited. Felicity wasn't quite sure what she was supposed to do.

"I asked you a question, Miss Murphy."

Still he was met with silence.

He got to his feet. The girl flinched, as if expecting attack. It was then Felicity saw the faint shadows along the side of her throat. Bruising. She looked more closely, but with long sleeves, it was impossible to tell if the girl had suffered more injuries.

"Who tried to choke you?" Felicity asked abruptly.

The girl flushed, then went dead white, her eyes huge in her thin face. Flint was staring at Felicity as if she'd lost her mind.

"You are safe here, Miss Murphy," Felicity promised.

Miss Murphy looked over at Flint, who sat back down.

"Yes," he said. "Absolutely safe. You were told you'd be safe here, weren't you?"

This time they at least got a small nod.

"And so you are. Are you going to America as well?"

The girl cast Felicity a look, then turned back to Lord Flint. She nodded.

"Why?" Another silence. A suspicion of tears in her eyes.

"You do know that I am the duke's son," Flint said, tapping fingers along his knee.

The girl looked frozen.

The rest of the interview didn't go any better.

"He really isn't a hard man," Felicity told the girl twenty minutes later after they'd been left alone with the tea things. "Sugar?"

The girl shook her head. Not a prosperous person then, whether servant or mistress, if she didn't want to give herself a taste of what she could never usually have. From the girl's faint accent, Felicity knew she'd come across the Irish Channel quite a while ago. From the calluses on her hands, Felicity would peg the girl as a servant. She handed over the cup into those shaking hands and poured her own, adding two lumps, not nearly as disciplined as the woman she faced. She *liked* sugar. She wanted to enjoy it while she could.

"You surprised Lord Flint," she explained as she stirred. "He had no idea this...er...program had been going on." Sipping at the lovely rich brew, she shrugged. "But then, he's rarely here, so I'm sure it hasn't mattered. Bad luck and timing for you."

Although why the duke hadn't foreseen the mischance Felicity couldn't think.

The girl sipped at the tea, and her eyes went wider. She looked down at the cup as if it should explain itself.

"Lovely, isn't it?" Felicity asked. "I must say that everyone is treated well here." When they weren't being harassed, anyway, to marry the heir for no better reason than he was handsome, funny, endearing and....well, the heir. The whole thing kept making less and less sense.

"You have been forbidden from speaking?" she asked the girl.

Again Miss Murphy looked around. Again she nodded.

"Do you *want* to go to America?"

This time the nod was enthusiastic and accompanied by a smile.

"I already have a situation," she admitted in the kind of gentle voice that should belong to the best of nannies. "In Boston. I have cousins there and all."

"It sounds marvelous," Felicity agreed and wondered if someone would like to offer her something similar.

Could Boston America be any worse than the wilds of Derbyshire? Maybe it was at least warmer there, so a person didn't get chilblains every time she removed her gloves at the piano.

"You'll not be...er, traveling with me?" the girl asked.

Felicity looked down at the sad state of her brown kerseymere and smiled. "Believe it or not," she said, "No. Although I begin to understand why even though she didn't speak much, Mrs. Windom fed me like the fatted calf."

"Truly?" There was deprivation in those magnificent blue eyes.

Felicity's smile grew. "Truly. What were you told of your stay here?"

"I keep to my room and everything would be delivered to me until such time as I leave to board my ship."

"Then so you shall. For a while at least, I seem to be in charge of the house, and I want you to feel safe. I have the most peculiar feeling you haven't in a while."

For which Pip would definitely demand answers of her uncle the duke if Felicity asked. Because there was no doubt about the sharp shadows that skimmed Miss Murphy's eyes.

Felicity gave a final nod. "How about this, Miss Murphy? That is an awfully small room you have, but we don't want it getting about to Lord Flint's aunt that you're here. She will torment you like a bluebottle fly. Not only that, evidently, she often has visitors. So, your universe will consist of your room and my sitting room. If you contain yourself thusly, I am certain you shall go unremarked."

Twenty minutes later Felicity checked for witnesses before ushering Nora Murphy back up to her room. And then Felicity headed back down to speak with Lord Flint.

She only made it as far as the second stair down from her own room. Before she made it another step, her legs simply seemed to give out on her and she found herself sitting on the step, her elbows on her knees, her chin in her hands, just staring at the graceful plaster acanthus leaves that rimmed the ceiling a story below.

She should continue on her way, she knew. Lord Flint would be waiting for her report, especially after she'd made such a point of ushering him out of her sitting room once it became apparent he wouldn't coax, bully or wheedle any more information from Miss Murphy. But too much had happened too quickly.

For the last four days all she had done was wander these rooms, ride around the park and once or twice take a turn at the duke's piano....

That reminded her. She had piano music somewhere. She had packed so fast to leave she'd completely forgotten to gather it up. She'd recover it when things settled down a bit.

Outside the tall windows the long gloaming had settled over the park, and below the servants were undoubtedly setting up for family dinner. Felicity had a feeling she truly should grab that music and run for her life while she had the chance. Nothing made sense to her, and the situation was growing odder by the moment. She simply didn't know what to do.

"Miss Chambers?" she heard above her.

Higgins, she realized.

"You poor man," she said, not moving. "Do you

ever get a moment off your feet?"

She thought he might have smiled. "It is rare the master is this busy here."

She smiled herself. "And yet you seem to have a steady stream of guests."

"Well, er...em...yes." She heard him rustle a bit, as if changing positions. "Is there anything I could get for you, Miss?"

She thought about asking him to join her on the step, but knew that the idea was a nonstarter. Good butlers would have to be missing both legs at the hip to sit in the presence of guests.

"I assume a maid comes with my fancy new bedroom?"

He cleared his throat. "As to that, Miss...the staff and I would like to—"

She lifted a finger in the air, still not facing him. "I had better not hear the word 'apologize,' Higgins. You forget. I have spent my adulthood caught between stairs, and I know precisely how this entire episode was mismanaged. And not by you or any of your staff."

It occurred to her at that moment that of course the staff would have known of the discussion in Aunt Winnie's sitting room. Poor Mrs. Windom must be gnawing her nails to the knuckle.

Felicity leaned her head far enough back to make eye contact with a very rigid Higgins. "Higgins," she said, gentling her own voice. "I would very much appreciate your delivering a message to Mrs. Windom as quickly as possible. She is an excellent housekeeper supervising a staff that is in good heart. Her job is quite secure."

Higgins didn't lower himself enough to actually

slump, but Felicity could see the hint of a smile. "You believe you might be remaining with us, Miss?" he asked in a suspiciously noncommittal voice.

Felicity returned her chin to her palms. "Oh, Higgins, I have no idea. But no matter what happens, I will make sure my promise to Mrs. Windom is kept."

"Thank you, Miss."

She nodded. "Now. That maid."

"Mrs. Windom had thought to appoint Sukie. Bright girl, ready for the chance."

Seventeen or so, just a bit taller than Felicity and plump as a berry scone, if memory served. *Hmmm,* Felicity thought. The idea of scones was making her stomach rumble. She was going to need to eat soon. "Could you ask her to join me, please?"

There was a brief pause. "Here?"

She grinned to herself. "Here, Higgins."

She thought he bowed. "At once, Miss."

Sukie ran, too. Everybody in this house seemed to have a habit of running, Felicity thought, still seated on her step.

The girl arrived from the servants' stairs at the back and trundled down the carpeted hallway.

"Yes, Miss Chambers?" she asked, stuttering to a halt at the top of the steps. "You needed me?"

Felicity patted the stair net to her. "Would you mind joining me, Sukie?"

This time the answering silence was longer. "There?"

Felicity just gave the step another pat.

"You've been appointed to do for me?" she asked when Sukie sat and tugged her skirts over the sturdy black shoes that pretty well-matched Felicity's own.

"If it please you, Miss. Yes."

Felicity finally sat up and turned to face her. "I am delighted, although I'm not sure how much you shall benefit. As you can see, I do not claim any pretensions to fashion. A good swipe of my shoes and warm water in the morning might be enough to do me. Is it enough for you?"

Sukie's smile was huge, revealing a bit of a gap between her two front teeth. "Lord love ya, Miss. I'll find somethin' to do. It's worth it for the advancement." Felicity nodded. That was right. Sukie had gained a better place at the servant's table with the promotion. Well, Felicity wasn't going to deny the girl her better ration and status.

"You can help me one way, if you will." Felicity took another look out over the staircase to where it swept down three more stories in an elegant oval. A far cry from anywhere she had ever lived before. And she was to be in charge of it, at least nominally. If she said yes, anyway.

"Anything, Miss."

"What do you know of Lord Flint?"

Sukie blushed and dipped her eyes. "Handsomest man in Gloucestershire."

"He is that."

"Not sure exactly what you want to know, Miss, since he's not here often."

"Where is he?" "Workin' for the duke, so I hear. Spent time travelin' and all. Was with the army chasin' Napoleon, too."

"And when he's here?"

Another flashing smile. "Most of the girls're half

in love with him. Can't help it, can they?" Her eyes widened abruptly. "Not me, o' course. I'm walking out with Jeb the groom. But everybody likes him."

"The staff is...er...comfortable with him?" "Do you mean does he bother the girls? Nobody bothers anybody here. He won't have it." She grinned suddenly. "And if he tried, Mrs. Windom would give him what how."

"And yet he has some rackety friends."

Sukie shrugged in the world-weary way of those in service. "All young men do, I'd say. And his could be worse. Noisy, mostly, a bit frolicsome, but only amongst themselves. There's no fear of being interfered with, which is a nice change, which I'm sure you know."

Felicity smiled. "I do indeed. It is why I fought to gain a slot in an all-girl's academy. Do you know anything about the girls who pass through here?"

Sukie wasn't stupid enough to miss the deliberate segue. "Nothin' more'n they need plumpin' up when they come. Silent as graves most of 'em. Glad to move on, though none'll have any complaints of their care here."

"If I'm any example, Sukie, that is definitely true."

"Are you truly going to be mistress of the house, Miss?"

Felicity turned back to her acanthus leaves. "I honestly don't know, Sukie. None of it makes sense to me."

Sukie laughed. "You'll pardon my sayin', Miss, but what difference does that make? Don't you want to live here? And above stairs?"

The truth? She did. She couldn't deny it. There

was something so lovely about the old bones of this place. Something homey and dear and loved that called to her lonely heart. Something that might just actually be hers, even for a while.

But as she well knew, as Sukie knew just as well, things were never that simple.

"What is the word downstairs?"

She was answered with silence.

"If I am to be mistress," Felicity said. "I need to know how to go on."

There was a small sigh. Felicity refused to face the girl, allowing her anonymity for the truth. "His lordship is much favored, Miss. And it hasn't gone unnoticed how good you were to Mrs. Windom."

Felicity nodded. "A good place to start, then. Thank you, Sukie. I appreciate the candor."

Sukie left the way she came. Felicity still couldn't work up the motivation to stand. She was caught dead center in the eye of a hurricane and didn't know how to navigate.

How could she? She was in an impossible place. A fantasy that made no sense. She had actually been whisked away from a second-rate boarding school at the invitation of a duke to meet his son with marriage in mind.

Marriage. To the son of a duke. Her, an orphan with a surname she had made up whole cloth.

And him....

She drew in an unforgivably trembly breath. Just thinking about him set those sparks loose again, spilling through her like fireworks and setting her limbs alight. Which didn't help her in the least. How could she keep a straight head while dealing with him when her body...when her body...?

She shook her head. It didn't even bear thinking about. If she couldn't control the rush of anticipation every time she thought of him, she would never be able to make a sensible decision.

That was troubling enough. In fact, it would have made an excellent plot for a Minerva Press novel. But then other women had been introduced to the plot. Frightened girls, really. Underfed, skittish, work-roughened girls on their way out of the country. Girls who were kept secret to all except for two men. Girls who had been hurt.

She had to believe that Lord Flint didn't know. He had truly looked as shocked as she felt. Sukie hadn't hesitated to defend him against any charges he might interfere with the help.

Felicity *wanted* to believe he was innocent of hurting the women who had moved through his house. She wanted to like him, she realized. He was unlike any of the aristocratic men she had known in her life, with the exception of Pip's brother Alex, who had helped rescue all the girls of Last Chance Academy back in the day.

Lord Flint could be completely overbearing. He could seem impervious to pressure, and rock stubborn against opposition. At the same time, he had apologized—-*apologized*—for having pressured her. She tried very hard to think of any other time in her life she had received an apology from anyone, much less the son of a duke, and simply could not.

Felicity sighed. She was in a dangerous place. She had known Lord Flint no more than a few hours, had known his intentions even fewer than that. And yet, she wanted them to be true. She wanted them to be honest. She wanted to think he liked her, too, and was sincere that he meant to make something out of his father's impossible demand.

And yet...

And yet, Felicity was too old to believe in fairy tales. If fairy tales were true, her parents would have come for her. They would have explained to her that they'd been lost at sea so long that by the time they looked she was beyond their reach. If fairy tales were real, she would have been a lost princess, not a teacher of ten-year-old girls who wanted no part of her, living in an unheated cubicle the size of Lord Flint's dining room table and using her half day off to bring her tatting into a local shop to sell for extra money.

If fairy tales were real, she wouldn't be alone. And Miss Murphy wouldn't have those bruises. And Aunt Winnie wouldn't live in hourly fear that she would lose the only world in which she still mattered.

Felicity knew she should leave. Sneak into her room, gather her meager belongings and tiptoe out the back door. Leave her sheet music if necessary. She should walk to Gloucester, all the way back to school if it came to it, if it meant being safely away from a situation that was looking more and more sketchy by the minute.

She should be strong enough to know better.

She feared very much that she wasn't.

There was nothing else for it. Taking hold of the banister, she pulled herself to her feet. It was time to move on. Pausing only long enough to brush any wrinkles from her feed sack of a dress, she sighed and continued on down the stairs.

CHAPTER 7

HE KNEW SHE WAS APPROACHING even before he heard the soft pad of her feet outside the library door. He knew before she knocked, before he bade her come in. It was the oddest thing. He'd asked her to join him, of course. He'd been waiting to hear if she had gained any more information from Miss Murphy.

But that wasn't why his head lifted seconds before the floorboard creaked at the far end of the corridor. Something shifted in him, something unsettling and new. Something he thought it would be wiser not to identify. Something that set his heart skidding and his cock waking.

Still, he put down the quill he'd been using to scratch a quick letter to his father and waited until he heard the sound of her knock.

"Come in."

Good lord, his palms were sweating. How could that be? He'd only met her that morning. There had been a spark of awareness when he'd taken her hand, of course, a delicious fire in her lips when he'd kissed her. But he'd felt that fire before and never actually anticipated seeing the woman again. Never looked forward to the surprise of learning just what she'd say next.

He definitely had to stop this now. Whatever his father expected of him, he suspected a real attraction wasn't part of it.

"Oh, you're busy," she said, stopping in the doorway.

She was such a little dab of a thing. How could he keep forgetting that? Maybe it was the rich color of her hair, like a good bay horse, or her eyes, that brown as deep as bitter chocolate. And she looked him in the eye. Nobody looked him in the eye. Not women, at least. It just wasn't done.

He found he liked it.

He glanced down at the half-finished letter. "I was just composing a threatening missive to the duke and a summons for my estate manager. Please. Sit down."

She approached as she might have an uncertain animal.

"Did you learn anything new from our guest?" he asked.

Felicity lowered herself onto the green leather chair across from him, her spine not quite touching the seatback. "She likes your tea."

He raised an eyebrow. "Indeed."

It would never do to let her know that he was relieved she'd joined him. He valued her level head, he assured himself, ignoring the smile that fought to rise in response to that pugnacious little chin, the sudden desire to pull a lock free from that tortured bun and see if it was as soft as it looked.

"Nothing else?" he asked instead.

"Nothing else. What do you plan to do now?"

"With Miss Murphy? Until I find out just what

is going on here, nothing. This all seems a bit too coincidental for my peace of mind."

Felicity used her palms to smooth out the lap of her dress, which seemed her only way of displaying nerves. "As I am not familiar with your father the duke, I couldn't offer an opinion. Does he frequently resort to subterfuge?"

Looking back down at the letter, Flint scowled. "Frequently. But usually only among my brothers and me."

Felicity looked up, frowning. "Why?"

He flashed on a memory of William, the oldest, lifting him by the scruff of his neck for the crime of laming his favorite hunter. William had damn near choked him, and it hadn't even been Flint who had been the culprit. But their father had intimated it just to see what would happen.

"He said conflict honed the senses," Flint mused, then considered the current situation. "But the older I get the more I suspect he simply can't help himself."

Another of his father's favorite themes had been that all it took to create unity among forces was a common enemy. Flint considered both his companion and the young woman upstairs and wondered if that was what his father was doing this time. Building a bond between him and Miss Chambers so she would come to trust him. Coincidence indeed.

Signing the brief missive to his father, he sanded it, affixed the wax seal and called Higgins to have a groom deliver it and the one to Mr. Everhill. Felicity waited patiently, her hands in her lap, questions boiling behind her eyes.

Flint gave himself enough time for Higgins to get well beyond eavesdropping range.

"So," he said, learning back and considering his guest, "we are not dismissing my housekeeper for insults to your person?"

Felicity dismissed the question with a small wave of her hand. "Don't be silly. You'd have to fire every servant who protected their place in the hierarchy, which would be a tad disingenuous from the son of a duke, don't you think?"

She wasn't precisely smiling, but there was a challenging sparkle in her eyes that settled very low in Flint's middle. He did love a sassy woman, especially in bed. Too bad he had other things to discover, which the events of the day had delayed far too much already.

"I would almost be forced to suspect you of enjoying yourself right now, Miss Chambers," he mused.

She outright grinned. "I do admit that repositioning small hands on piano keys does not afford quite so much enjoyment as..." She tilted her head, considering. "What exactly would you call today? A carnival? A challenge? A mayhem?"

"Since you have been involved," he said, "a delight."

Good. He got a blush out of her, mild but definite. It made the faint scattering of freckles over her nose stand out. He hated freckles. But somehow, he didn't hate these. Not at all.

While he was musing on Miss Chambers' more interesting attributes, she rose to her feet. "If there is nothing else you require of me," she said, "I shall retreat to my room."

Once again he was surprised, this time by disappointment. He deliberately maintained his place. "Miss Chambers, you don't have to ask my leave. You don't work for me."

She gave her head a little tilt. "A difficult habit to break. Especially since I am still unsure exactly what my position is here."

At that he rose. "You are my fiancée."

She gave her head a quick shake. "Not until I say yes. If I do."

Flint nodded. Nothing else he could do. "Well then, you are my guest."

"With housekeeping duties."

"With the rights of a lady of the house."

She just frowned. "And your aunt? I will effectively displace a woman who has had a free hand here for how long?"

He shrugged. "Gran's been gone two years."

She nodded. "At least allow me to accord her the respect to maintain some of her control."

He considered her a moment. How many other women would offer to share seniority? "You are now in charge of the house. It is your decision."

She gave him another quick, firm nod.

"I'll see you at dinner?"

Her eyebrows rose. "Will you?"

He shook his head. "My fiancée does not eat in the kitchen."

"But I am not your fiancée."

He was frowning now, even though he was enjoying the bright edge of her wit. "Call yourself what you wish," he said. "You will eat with me. In the dining room. Like a civilized person. Maybe we can start to get to know each other."

"And your aunt?"

He grinned at her. "God only knows."

His aunt did join them, perched upon a fat pillow placed with an almost reverent attention by Miss Fare, who took the seat next to her. Felicity decided it was probably better that the old woman had joined them. She was feeling jittery again, unbalanced, as if Lord Flint was yanking the carpet from under her feet. She worried about what kind of conversation she would be obliged to enter and what deficiencies in form and manner she might betray.

Instead she listened to a desultory conversation that mostly involved people and places Felicity had no knowledge of, which left her ample time to enjoy the luxury of a civilized meal where little hands weren't spilling things and little voices weren't raised in ear-splitting whines.

It didn't bother her at all that she knew few of the people involved, although it did amaze her at the number who regularly saw their way to Glenhaven to visit, and of all generations. No wonder Aunt Winnie knew so much about so many.

But that was not a problem she decided to waste time on. The wine was beyond anything she had ever tasted. The food was delicious enough that she had to remind herself not to squirrel any away in her pockets for later when she would certainly be hungry. No one went hungry in a duke's house, even an impecunious instructor of piano and deportment.

Maybe one small apple, she thought, instincts

pushing her hard as she watched Flint and his aunt discuss several men he had served with. *Perhaps a boiled potato. Just in case. No one would notice, surely.*

"Are you expecting sudden famine, Miss Chambers?" Lord Flint asked, his voice dry as dust.

Felicity dropped the small, warm potato into her pocket and lifted her chin. "It is a long walk to the kitchens, my lord. Sometimes a person gets a mite peckish later on."

He lifted a quizzing glass. An actual gold quizzing glass, as if she were an insect to be examined. "From the way your dress hangs, your peckishness must be chronic."

She felt a miserable flush rise up her neck. As if she needed to hear that she had only recently had an even plumper figure.

"I may not be an expert, my lord," she said, keeping her chin high, "but I believe that such a comment is not considered appropriate courting behavior."

He lifted one eyebrow, which made Felicity even more unhappy. She had practiced for months to affect such a look. She had never succeeded. There was something so wonderfully toplofty about it, especially when the person wielding it was wearing his best dinner attire.

"I don't know," he said, dropping the glass and picking up his wine. "I would think that if one were so chronically under-served as to pilfer dinner victuals, any man who could provide an unlimited supply of potatoes would seem quite attractive."

An odd gurgle escaped her. Damn him, he truly made her laugh, even over her own humiliation.

"You are not going to shame me into putting

that potato back," she challenged. "You can have no idea what it means."

And that quickly, the entire tone of the conversation changed. "What *does* it mean?" he asked softly.

And Felicity was caught on the barb of her own hook. How did she make him understand without further diminishing her in his eyes? How to retain her dignity when speaking of long cold nights with a gnawing stomach, of locked doors and cabinets that kept staff and students away from the food, no matter how unpalatable it was. How could she make him understand want without making herself a pitiable figure?

Briefly she looked away, only to discover the paper-thin defiance in the expression of Aunt Winnie, iron-straight, hands clenched on the table. And Felicity knew that at least one other person understood. Not the food perhaps, but the desperation.

"It is about," she finally said, turning back to Lord Flint, "the tyranny of uncertainty."

For a long moment, there was silence. Even Lord Flint seemed to have nothing to say. Felicity held her breath, wanting him to understand without having to give anything else away. She could only bear to diminish herself in his eyes so much.

"What an excellent idea," Aunt Winnie suddenly barked. "Pass me that bowl of potatoes, gel. Miss Fare might be hungry later."

Again, Felicity almost laughed, this time from relief. God bless the old tartar. And Miss Fare, who accepted the bowl from Aunt Winnie and, smiling, slipped a single potato into her pocket.

Lord Flint watched them all, and then leaned back in his chair, sipping at his wine. "The only difference between you and me," he said, "is that my uncertainty will never involve food."

Felicity didn't have the courage or the energy to withstand another grilling over tea. The minute Aunt Winnie excused the ladies from the table, she attempted to excuse herself from company and head up to bed.

"Not yet," the old woman said, making her way down the hall at a surprising speed for someone who leaned heavily on a silver-topped cane. "You will join us."

She joined them, perching onto a royal blue brocade chair, back rigid, hands in lap as she taught her students to do, and she waited for Aunt Winnie to be settled on the powder-blue settee.

"Well," Aunt Winnie declared with a thump of her cane, thankfully on an Aubusson carpet. "You didn't disgrace yourself, at least."

It was moments like this Felicity so wished she could lift one eyebrow. Maybe if she married Lord Flint, she would get a quizzing glass just like his so she could lift it to one eye. Surely that would create the same impression.

Instead she sat still and waited, refusing to give the old woman the satisfaction of making her explain herself.

Another thump. "I was thinking at dinner. You went to that school with Phillipa."

"I did." Although she suspected Pip wouldn't recognize herself by that name.

Out of the corner of her eye she saw Miss Fare take a seat by the window and pick up her needlework.

"Why?" Aunt Winnie demanded.

Felicity blinked, turning back. She had obviously missed something. "Why what?"

"Why did you go there? Very select school. Couldn't go without a recommendation. Who recommended you?"

Again, Felicity was reduced to blinking. She had never thought about it.

"I don't understand."

Aunt Winnie blew out a frustrated breath. "Miss Chase's isn't just for any parvenu who decides she wants to ape her betters. It *is* for betters. Many daughters of government men go there. How did you get in?"

Felicity tried to remember back far enough to answer. But she couldn't recall actually moving from the country house to the school. She had been about six, she thought, and all she could remember of those first months at the academy was cold, hunger, loneliness and the surprising balm of the written word. She had soaked up language like a proverbial sponge and read everything she could get hold of, which admittedly wasn't much at first.

But it had been her only joy, her companion in the empty nights when other girls not much older than she kept away.

Until Pip. Pip had changed her entire world.

"I truly don't know, ma'am," she said. "I never thought about it. One day I was in the country, and the next locked in that awful place."

Aunt Winnie's frown grew more ferocious, which

made the gentle tone of her voice a surprise. "It was unconscionable what you girls went through. I heard about it from Pip's father, the dolt. Leave it to men to drop you off and simply assume you were safe. No one ever came to visit you?"

Felicity shook her head. Safe? Who would have ever thought anybody could be safe under the auspices of Miss Chase? For the longest time Felicity had thought she was being punished for something.

Aunt Winnie nodded her head once, sharply. "Well, at least they taught you to be a lady. It will be easier passing you off."

Felicity decided that she had had quite enough. "You needn't pass me off," she said and stood. "I *am* a lady."

And with a quick bob of a curtsy, she turned and walked out.

She was halfway down the hall when she heard another crack of laughter. "She'll need every bit of that spine for what's coming, if I'm any judge."

Oh, excellent, Felicity thought, trudging up the stairs. That was just the encouragement she needed.

Lord Flint hadn't merely assigned her a room, she admitted as she stepped back into the brightly-decorated sitting room connected to her bedroom. He had provided her a sanctuary. And if Aunt Winnie was correct, she was going to need it.

Just to make sure the rooms really were a sanctuary, she turned the key to the hallway and locked the door. Then she walked through to her bedroom and locked that door too. She wasn't quite sure why it was so important. She thought Sukie was correct. She did not risk injury in this house. Even so, it might just be wiser to make sure nothing intruded on her peace. Especially a too-handsome almost-fiancé with the most delicious dimples she had ever encountered.

Making one more test of the locked door, she finally relaxed and turned back to her bed. Which was when she realized how bone-tired she was. Too much running about today, too much uncertainty and surprise. Too much emotion—panic, anger, grief, hope, caution—all in one day. Heavens, she hadn't allowed herself that many emotions since she'd graduated from Last Chance and stepped out into the world. It simply didn't pay to let yourself be that vulnerable.

Sukie had obviously already been in the room. Felicity's worn, white cotton night rail was carefully laid out on the turned-down bed. Felicity thought she had never seen anything so inviting in her life.

Oh, and there underneath was her music. Mozart's "Turkish March" from *Sonata 11*, the perfect piece for limbering up proficient fingers. She wondered where the staff had found it. They wouldn't have bothered with something sitting on the piano, which was where she'd thought she'd left it.

She shrugged. Oh well. At least she had it back. She would simply need to remember to collect it from her room next time she practiced.

Picking up the sheets, she slipped them into the dresser drawer. Then she reached around to untie her dress and couldn't help grinning. She bumped into two separate lumps in her pocket. A potato and a roll. Just in case. Pulling them both out, she hid them behind the clock on her bureau. Then she finished readying herself for sleep.

Flint was standing in the wrong hallway. He knew that. His rooms were in the west wing. This was the north. But when he saw Miss Chambers stalk out of the sitting parlor, he instinctively followed a ways behind, wanting to make sure she was all right.

He had just reached the door to her sitting room when he heard the lock close with a very definitive *click*. It stopped him with his hand raised to knock. Should he knock anyway and demand to know what was wrong? To see whether his aunt needed some taking down?

Another lock clicked from the bedroom door to his left. He found himself smiling. If that wasn't a statement, then he didn't know what was.

And yet, still he didn't leave. He could hear her moving about in her room, soft whispers of fabric and softer mutterings. He imagined her readying herself for bed, pulling out those medieval torture devices that held her hair back until it flowed down her back, thick and shiny and touchable. Did it curl or fall straight as a waterfall? Would she sit to brush it or simply weave it into a braid? Would it feel like silk in his hands?

And then that misshapen nightmare of a frock. What really lurked beneath? He knew she had curves. But in what proportion? Did she wear stays? Were her hips as lush as they seemed, a fair match for her pert breasts?

"Seduce her if you must," his father had said.

Suddenly the idea had merit. His body certainly

thought so. Just the thought of having those delicious breasts in his hands had him hard as a stone.

He frowned and turned away. Too bad he still had a semblance of a conscience. It would have been one thing to seduce somebody like Gen, who knew the rules and would have participated with enthusiasm. Felicity Chambers did not. Not only that, she did not hold the kind of position in society that would buffer her from condemnation

The terrorism of uncertainty. And he was about to make it worse. He didn't have to make it that much worse.

CHAPTER 8

Two days later

"WHERE IS YOUR RIDING HABIT?"

Felicity looked up from the last of her morning eggs. "Why yes, it is a lovely morning, thank you."

He had been away the day before, seeing to some problem with a local dam. It seemed odd that he would disappear right after making such a point of her staying, but she imagined unexpected things happened on estates just as much as in cities. She had filled her own time getting to know the staff and deciding which responsibilities she would temporarily take over and which to leave to Aunt Winnie.

She was actually amazed how much she'd enjoyed it. How comfortable she felt slipping into a role she had trained for and never expected to occupy. It was foolish, but she couldn't help growing even more attached to Hedgehog Haven and all its denizens.

And then, to secure her regard more surely than any gift might have, she had claimed the music room. A grand harp stood in the corner of the quietly classical ivory and burgundy room. The lovely pianoforte took up the window, out which she could see the pastureland rolling away to the wood. Reclaiming the sheet music from her room, she closed the door and spent several hours losing herself in Mozart. The rest of her world might be in upheaval, but Mozart's precision and emotion calmed her more surely than tea and biscuits.

When she got to the end of his *Sonata 11*, she turned the page to find an extra sheet. Taking a quick look, she decided it was a practice sheet from one of her students. She shook her head. Undoubtedly Mary Tracy. The girl had even less of an eye for music than she did for mathematics.

Felicity had planned on returning to Mozart after breakfast this morning. From the looks of Lord Flint, she wasn't going to make it.

He was standing in the doorway frowning. "My apologies. I didn't mean to leave you alone all day yesterday. So, I thought you might like to go out with me this morning. If you'll don your habit..."

Straightening against the discomfort those words produced, she shook her head. "I have none."

Flint stepped further into the breakfast room. "But you've ridden."

"I have. Billie is teaching me." In fact, after luncheon yesterday, he had let her trot around the paddock until her bottom ached.

"In what?"

She sighed. There would be no leisurely cup of tea to be savored while contemplating the view out over the back parterre. No extra crumpet or visit with Herr Mozart. Lord Flint was tapping his crop against his buckskin breeches.

Felicity desperately wished he didn't look so compelling standing there in those form-fitting breeches, the glossy tasseled boots, the gentleman's coffee-colored jacket and mathematical knot in his neckcloth. His clothing merely emphasized the strength and elegance of his form. His coat perfectly fit his broad shoulders. It softened his chiseled features not at all. Nor did it sap the power of his eyes, which gleamed spring green in the morning sunlight.

Blast him for being every girl's fantasy.

She held her arms out to her sides. "This is what I wear. Since I have only been riding about your estate, it did not seem quite so outrageous that my half-boots showed a bit."

He dragged his hand through his hair, completely destroying the Brutus cut his valet had obviously spent time on. "You...I thought you had ridden the paddocks."

"No. I did go farther afield." She tilted her head. "Oh, I see. If I went that far, why didn't I simply keep riding? Because Mr. Burke was attached to me like a cocklebur, that's why. Besides, he would have been blamed for my escape, and I did not wish him to be punished. He has been most kind to me."

Lord Flint's attention wandered even as he gave a vague nod. "I was thinking of touring the farms today."

She nodded. "They have been anxious to see you."

That reclaimed his attention. "You've *seen* them?"

Another moment for a lifted eyebrow, Felicity thought. "They are on the property. And Mr. Burke likes to stop in regularly. I believe I like the Fosters the best. They have a lovely new baby with bright red hair. And Mrs. Foster

bakes the most delicious currant scones. You might want to check on the thatching, though. It's a bit spotty."

Felicity deliberately smiled. Flint was looking more thunderous by the second.

"What would a deportment teacher know about thatching?" he demanded.

"She would know when rain plops on her nose while being served scones in a kitchen."

"I'll get you an interview with the duke," he growled. "I'm certain he would be delighted to know you have everything well in hand."

"I should be happy to instruct him."

Popping the last bit of crumpet into her mouth, Felicity got to her feet. Her frock today was another disaster, a moss-green Circassian cloth with long sleeves and a bit of worn lace about the collar. Not very attractive as a dress or a habit. At least it was heavy and long enough to protect her modesty on a side saddle.

"Shall we go?" she asked, giving her skirts a final brush-off as she joined him at the door.

He didn't answer, just turned and preceded her down the corridor to get her bonnet and spencer and exit the house.

The stable block was set behind the kitchen, a sturdy brick C that housed a dozen healthy denizens including Flint's matched carriage grays and the stallion he had ridden down, a massive chestnut with a bright eye. Billy Burke was standing in the yard between the stallion and the sleepy-looking black Felicity had been riding.

Her horse nudged her shoulder and was rewarded with a lump of sugar. The stallion alongside nickered and stretched out his neck to receive his own. Felicity chuckled at the imperious look in his eye.

"Now you're making up to my horse?" Flint demanded.

"I have discovered that horses are often superior acquaintances to humans," she said, letting the chestnut lip the sugar from her palm. "What is his name?"

"Don't they have any horses at that school where you teach?"

Felicity accepted a leg up and settled herself atop Charlie who seemed as tall as the manor house balcony. "No. It is not a rich enough school."

Besides, she had never had enough extra time to learn even if they had had horses. Or a riding instructor. If she had, she might have already known that fear can sometimes be exhilarating.

"Your posts before?"

She patted Charlie's neck and settled reins and crop. "I was not in a position to learn to ride there."

She had been invited. But the price for a few minutes' canter would have come far too high.

Lord Flint vaulted into his saddle with effortless grace and settled the great animal with a few soft words and a gathering of reins.

"Galahad," he said.

Felicity looked up, surprised. "Pardon?"

He actually looked uncomfortable. "Galahad. The horse's name."

This time Felicity thought she might have

gaped. "Why, Lord Flint," she accused. "You are a romantic!"

He huffed impatiently. "Don't be absurd. That was his name when I bought him."

Out of the corner of her eye Felicity caught a passing expression on Billy Burke's face that made her think she was being lied to. She might have challenged Lord Flint on his statement if she hadn't thought she would put him in such a snit that he would cancel the ride.

"Lord Flint..."

"Bracken," he barked, guiding his horse to her side. "You don't have to Lord Flint me all the time. My last name is perfectly acceptable."

Felicity tilted her head a bit. "So, my choice is between an incendiary rock or a prickly weed. I don't suppose there are any other names to choose from. Otter, Fieldstone, Toadstool?"

His scowl, she admitted, was magnificent. It only increased when Billy Burke let out a huffing laugh. "How do you ever keep a position with a tart mouth like that?" Flint demanded.

She gave him her brightest smile, buoyant with the realization that she never had felt secure enough anywhere to be herself. Anywhere but with Pip. And, evidently, here.

"I never waste my smart mouth on employers. Only fictitious fiancés."

It was Flint's turn to huff. "Just my luck."

Without another word, he wheeled Galahad about and set him off down the lane. Felicity had the feeling it was his way of maintaining the upper hand. She didn't mind, at least for the moment. She got to be on a horse out in the fresh air. Nothing else mattered. With a final smile at the laughing stablemaster, she turned after Flint.

Oh, dear. He was galloping off as if she would follow. She had barely gotten past a posting trot in her lessons. And Charlie was pulling on the reins to follow the much larger horse.

Suddenly Billy let out a shrill whistle. Flint pulled Galahad up to a gravel-scrunching stop and turned back.

"Oh!" he called. "Sorry."

Felicity had the feeling that he didn't mean it, but she quite understood. The morning was brisk with an early autumn breeze, the plane trees that lined the drive just beginning to yellow in a weak sun. She wished she could just gallop off after him.

Settling the gelding to a trot to catch up, Felicity drew in a great lungful of air, savoring the mingled scents of grass and leaf mold and country. It had been one of the benefits of this last six days, reacquainting herself with the rhythms and simplicity of the countryside. No matter what else happened in her life, the countryside soothed her.

She had hoped to go out on her own this morning, too, give herself some distance in which to contemplate what was going on. A nice quiet ride with Mr. Burke to clear her head. Instead she was following Lord Flint from the yard and wondering what he had in mind.

Fortunately, he must have felt the same way she did.

"Would you like to try a canter?" he asked as she pulled up, Charlie slowing after him like a gentleman.

She would like nothing better. And yet, suddenly

a canter seemed far too fast and high. She'd managed it twice, right alongside Mr. Burke, and felt as if she'd fly right off the tiny saddle. And yet, now seemed the perfect chance to try again.

So, she nodded and curled her leg more tightly around the horn, afraid she was becoming addicted to the tight-chested attraction of risk. Flint grinned and set Galahad off. Charlie followed right behind. And Felicity failed to fall off.

The exhilaration of it crowded her throat. Too fast. She was going too fast. She knew it. Too high and too fast. And yet suddenly she found the rhythm of the gait and leaned into it, like settling into a rocking chair. It was just what she'd dreamed riding a horse would be. She curled her knee more tightly yet and made sure the reins were taut and her posture straight.

Felicity had no idea where they were going. They were headed in the opposite direction Mr. Burke usually took. It didn't matter. She all but laughed at the feeling of flight. She loved the sense of sudden freedom, as if the earth fell away beneath Charlie's hooves. She loved the jangle of the tack and the creak of the leather and the pull and ease of the reins through her fingers.

Charlie didn't have the stallion's size or power, but he was as game as a pebble. He followed right behind the bigger horse as they crossed the fields, clods of dirt kicking up in their wake. If she could, she would run like this forever. She and Charlie would take flight just to see how long they could go, how far behind they could leave their troubles and questions. All the way to John O'Groats, if necessary.

They were approaching a village Felicity didn't recognize. They had been heading southwest away from Edgecombe, the estate village, and crossed a bridge or two. Breaking through the tree line, Flint turned them onto a road that wound through harvested fields towards a group of old brick-and-half-timbered buildings clustered along an abnormally long village green. Swans circled a pond at the near end, and at the other, the road wandered off amid the horse chestnuts that ringed a square church steeple.

Just as they reached the first houses, Flint eased back on his mount. Felicity followed suit, giving Charlie another few pats for his service.

"Where are we?" she asked, breathless from the ride.

They had eased to a walk, Lord Flint falling back to ride alongside. "Frampton-on-Severn," he said, pointing to the square Norman steeple that peeked through the trees. "That is St. Mary the Virgin. First stone laid down in the 1100s."

It took Felicity a moment to follow his guidance as she quickly stuffed her wayward hair back into its pins. Thankfully Charlie seemed to know the way.

"What an interesting place," Felicity mused, her attention caught by all the ancient brick and half-timbering, the air of sleepy disuse that seemed to envelop the road. "Is there any building newer than a hundred years old?"

"I don't believe so. Do you see the green?"

It would have been difficult to miss it. There was no real high street, no square of any kind. Just that long stretch of cropped grass, which didn't seem to contain much activity at present.

"I do."

"Do you know why the green is this long?"

"Of course, I do," she said, giving a final pat to her hair and tightening the reins a bit. "Although I've rarely seen one maintained this long. It was the law in the Middle Ages. The green had to extend the length of a long-bow shot, so the local yeomanry could practice."

Flint shook his head. "How would an instructor of piano and deportment know that?"

She couldn't help smiling. "The instructor reads history for her own pleasure, which she learned from your cousin. Pip was always spouting off things like that. Anything to do with the courtly age, knights in shining armor, quests, Crusades. She was enamored."

"I believe the word you're looking for is obsessed. Drove us mad with her quests for holy grails when we were young."

Felicity smiled. "She told me."

Felicity had listened in rapt attention to what she'd always considered fairy stories of close-knit families and the kind of cousins who abused and amused each other with the nonchalance of familiarity. Adventure amid safety, the easy assumption that one belonged somewhere.

She had listened to Pip from her place in that hard gray dormer bed, envying the bright comforters and knitted throws the other girls had brought from home to keep them warm. Part of the fairy story of belonging.

Flint guided his horse to a small, red-brick inn and dismounted. Striding around to Felicity's side, he reached up without a word and caught her at the waist. Felicity started badly. The last time a man had caught her in such a way, he had forced her to stomp on his feet to get free. But the feeling wasn't the same now. Not at all. When Flint set her down on the ground, she caught herself just short of leaning into him, simply to enjoy the scent of sandalwood and man. Her skin still tingled after he took his hand away. Her knees felt a bit fluid. She quickly stepped away and smoothed down her skirts.

Flint acted as if he hadn't even noticed. Instead he pointed with his crop toward a manor house down the way that was part mellow red brick and part half-timber. "Did she tell you about the Manor?"

Felicity turned to look in the direction he indicated.

He was gazing on the time-softened house with a smile. "The Fair Rosamund was born there. Mistress to Henry II and bane of Queen Eleanor's existence."

Felicity gaped. "*That* is the Manor?" She shook her head, reconsidering what she saw. "My heavens. I have certainly heard enough about it. Pip has never liked poor Rosamund, you know. She is a staunch Eleanor supporter."

"Pip is nothing if not loyal."

"Would that Henry had been."

Flint's smile grew. "Eleanor was no weeping violet herself."

"And why should she be? She had power. She used it."

Flint laid a hand at her back, causing her to startle a bit. "I can see that I'll have to keep constant watch for attempted insurrection," he said as he guided her through the door of the little ale house that was so low he was forced to duck.

They entered a dark, smoky taproom with a few listing tables and a well-worn bar. Across the flagstone floor a pair of farmers sat at a battered table nursing ales. A pretty blond barmaid leaned on the counter, thinking her own thoughts.

Flint seated Felicity at a table by the front window and set down his crop on the table.

"Tea?" he asked her.

"Ale."

Up went that eyebrow. "Indeed."

"The samples I've had in the neighborhood have been quite good," she assured him, reaching up to untie her bonnet. "In fact, your own estate ale is a recipe from Aunt Winnie."

Flint stopped in his tracks. "Aunt Winnie?"

Felicity smiled. "She has been in charge of its brewing since she's been here. I hope you don't mind that I asked her to continue."

"You had that talk, did you?"

"Yes. And it was astonishingly amicable. I think we should get along famously." His eyebrow began to rise. Felicity raised her finger in response. "If I stay."

There was something so satisfying about making him huff like that. She had a feeling no one else dared try, except maybe the Siren. Felicity admitted that it gave her a rather delicious shiver to see the spark flare in his eyes.

By the time he returned, her bonnet was on the table and her gaze out onto the long green. "So, if that is the Manor down the lane," she mused, "then this must be Rosamund Green?"

He set two brimming mugs down on the table and took up the other chair. "It is."

She nodded, peering out through the thick glass to the village beyond. "Pip really does love this place. I'm glad I saw it."

"You could live near it," he coaxed. "Possibly invite Pip to wander all over it with you and tell you the local stories."

Refusing to betray the pain that offer ignited, Felicity just smiled and picked up her ale.

"It is my concerted belief," she said after taking a long sip and surreptitiously wiping the foam from her upper lip, "that men conspire to keep the better things away from women."

He looked around. "Like what, the green? The alehouse?"

"The ale."

Flint's chair scraped across the stone as he picked up his own ale and leaned back. "Most women aren't interested in things like ale."

"Most women have never been given the chance to decide for themselves."

"So, you're doing it for them?"

She tilted her head. "It has been a long few days."

"I thought you spent it locked in the house with no one to talk to."

"Metaphorically speaking."

He gave a mournful shake of the head. "I don't suppose this behavior is an aberrancy."

She considered it. "Well. Of course, I haven't had the latitude to try ale or jump fences in my various positions. It might severely impact the morals of the children. God forbid they should learn to stand up for themselves or, perish the thought, have adventures."

"Please tell me you were this radical before arriving here. It would serve my father right."

She flashed him a bright grin. "I was one of Pip's best pupils in revolutions and rambunctiousness."

"It must frustrate you now being so constrained."

Felicity's smile faded. She shook her head and took another sip, savoring the dry, nutty taste of the brew. "Not eating frustrates me far more."

For a long moment, there was just silence punctuated by the soft murmurs from the other men, two rosy-cheeked grandfathers in tweed caps and hard boots.

"You truly never found out who your people were?" Flint asked, his gaze on his glass.

Felicity looked up, surprised. "No. Pip says I have a perverse streak. I have decided that if they do not wish to know me, I am happy to return the favor."

He went very still. "What if they don't know you exist?"

She shrugged, trying to ignore the familiar ache in her chest. "Pip looked in the school records once. Said there was nothing there. I was actually a bit relieved. I cannot imagine how uncomfortable it would have been to show up on some toff's doorstep crying, 'Mother!'"

She knew she had disconcerted him. He went quiet, staring into his ale as if scrying his future. For the first time in a long while, Felicity felt uncomfortable herself about her situation. She shouldn't. It had never been a secret. Somehow, though, sitting in this homely little inn across from such a handsome man, she wanted to be more than she was. Actually worthy of his consideration instead of merely a chore.

A chore. She unconsciously shook her head. The story of her life.

"How many positions *have* you had?" he asked, not looking up.

She looked at his hands—long, elegant fingers, strong wrists, with a scar or two marring the knuckles. Lovely hands. The hands of a gentleman who had known work.

"Three," she said, turning back to her glass. "Two as governess and one at the school. That would be the one your father the duke undoubtedly destroyed for me."

"Is marriage to me truly a worse prospect than teaching piano to snot-nosed little girls?"

She straightened, desperately trying to inject a bit of humor. "I will have you know that our little girls were all perfectly groomed and behaved… well, the last might be a bit of a stretch."

His smile was quiet. "So am I. Am I so terrible a prospect?"

"You are an unknown prospect. Remember. I didn't know of you until four days ago."

"Of course, you did," he protested, tapping his chest. "I'm Igneous."

"Igneous was a twelve-year old who played Knights of the Round Table and loved kippers. You are…" She gave him a quick, assessing look. "Not."

This time his grin was brash. "I'm far better."

"In what way? And please contain your answer to one that can be repeated in your aunt's parlor. The last I heard about you, you were leaving for the army in a magnificent red coat and shako, a lovely woman hanging off each arm."

He surprised her. Instead of throwing off a blithe answer, he frowned. Suddenly his hands became restless, and he seemed fascinated by the handle of his mug.

"Bracken?" she asked quietly.

He gave her a quick, rueful smile. "I was quite the sight, if I do say so myself. It seems uniforms imbue one with a very inflated sense of one's self-worth. It was the career I was given as third son—certainly more fitting than vicar, which my older brother Ransom was given—and I was well pleased."

"Has the romance of it paled?" she asked.

"Nothing so gentle. War is not all perfectly-tailored parade jackets and glossy boots. It is crashing boredom and flashes of abject terror. What surprised me was that I resented the boredom far worse than the terror."

Suddenly he looked up, his eyes wide. Startled, as if he'd overheard his own words for the first time. Felicity didn't know what to do. She found herself wanting to reach out and hold him. At least to lay her hand over his so he wasn't alone with that admission.

He broke the mood with a laugh and a shake of his head. "Can you be too good at an occupation? God bless Grandmother for giving me a different direction for my talents."

Felicity tilted her head. "How does a talent for mayhem help an estate?"

"A talent for organization and planning. I have many, many plans for the Haven."

"If only your father will release it."

"Yes. If only that."His admission did nothing to ease the growing tumult in her chest. She didn't want to be his answer. She didn't want him to require nothing more than her name on a form so he could gain his inheritance.

On the other hand, how else could she ever expect to have a family of her own? And she did want one. It was a dream she had kept carefully tucked away with her saved shillings and the whitework she had so painstakingly practiced to include in her trousseau. The trousseau her classmates had all already used while hers languished untouched at the bottom of her trunk.

"What do you expect?" she asked suddenly.

He looked up, startled. "Of what?""Marriage. What exactly are you hoping for?" She gave her hand a little wave. "Besides the estate, of course. From me. What do you expect from me?"

She wasn't certain how she expected him to respond. She should have known he'd surprise her. It was he who reached out and curled his fingers around her hand. It was he who stole her breath with just the brush of his skin.

"What do *you* want?" he asked, those soft green eyes intense.

What did she *want?* She wanted to remember how to breathe again. She wanted enough space to actually consider what he was asking of her. What he was offering. She *wanted* to not be backed into a decision that would change her whole life.

"A voice," she said, surprised at the admission, not the breathy quality of her own voice.

He stared at her a moment."A voice?"

Briefly she squeezed her eyes shut. She was about

to offer up the desire she'd tucked away even below the dream of a family. She was about to share it with a man she didn't know, not really. Only really being acquainted with him a day, she was entrusting him with the only dream that had never died.

CHAPTER 9

THIS WASN'T WHAT FLINT MEANT to be talking about at all. He was supposed to be talking of her last governess position. The people she'd known, things she might have overheard. Instead he was sitting here waiting for her to tell him a truth he suspected she didn't want to tell and he didn't want to hear. He was rubbing his thumb over her slightly-callused palm that should have been satin soft and somehow was more appealing for not being so, waiting for her to confirm his suspicion that she had been dragged into a conspiracy that wasn't hers.

"A voice?" he prompted, knowing he was heading down the wrong road.

And yet, he wanted to know what that hesitation in her giant brown eyes meant.

As if hearing his thoughts, she looked away to where the barmaid was flirting with one of the old men at the table. It was harmless, sweet even. The barmaid had the old codger blushing with her bright, easy smile. It was the kind of familiar interplay that happened between people who knew each other well. Who knew where they belonged in the village, in the nation, in the world.

Flint lived in just that kind of world. Even if he didn't know the people with whom he interacted personally, he knew, and more importantly they knew, exactly where he belonged in the hierarchy. He was a duke's son and accorded appropriate respect. He was a brother who knew exactly where he fit in the family. He could insult his brothers at will and know he'd get a cuffing and a grin. He was an Eton man, a Balliol man, a member of Whites, Brooks, Gentleman Jackson's and the Coldstream Guards, and knew exactly how he would be treated in all those places. Whom he should ignore or invite closer. Whom he owed respect and by whom he was owed it.

What, he thought, would it be like to never know? How would someone navigate the shoals of society when she had been given no more than a ticket to a boarding school where all the other girls knew their place? How did she overcome the— what had she called it?—terror of uncertainty?

"Felicity?"

She looked up, and that quickly the shadows fled. Flint had a feeling the act was deliberate.

She smiled. "Oh," she said, gently pulling her hand free, "I suppose the easiest way to put it is that I would far rather not be the supplicant in my own marriage."

Flint almost gaped at her. God, who was this woman, and where did she come by such knife-edge awareness? How did she have the courage to speak it out loud?

"You think I would hold my offer over your head?"

"Many would."

He thought his smile was probably a bit rueful. "But I am Igneous."

"You are also still the son of the Duke of Lynden. I am—"

He waved off the rest of that sentence. "Yes, yes. So you have been at pains to tell me. Are you afraid of being silenced because you have so little to say, or so much?"

This time her smile grew. "Oh, so much. Definitely so much."

"But I like women who speak up."

"Even if they challenge your decisions and rights?"

He paused for a moment that stretched out almost uncomfortably. "It seems to me that you're making it a point to list all the detriments to marrying you. I don't believe any other woman would do that."

"It is difficult enough to be invisible among society. It would be soul-crushing among those to whom I entrust my life." Her frown returned. "Which brings us back to the inevitable question. Why me? What exactly do I bring to a marriage with the son of a duke?"

He attempted his own grin. "Piano and deportment?"

Her frown, if anything, grew. "Not very much of a dowry."

"To be perfectly frank, I don't provide much more."

"Your house."

"I consider that to be a gift from both of us. If I don't marry, I will lose it for another five years. And the duke has promised to let it languish, just to tighten the screws a bit."

"Excellent," she mused darkly. "Matrimony by extortion."

"I do mean to make it a great success."

"I don't doubt you at all. I don't doubt that you can make anything you wish a success."

Flint felt as if he'd taken a blow to the gut. His skin actually went clammy. "That would not necessarily be a safe bet, my dear."

She looked up, the bemusement clear in her eyes.

He kept his smile small. "Do you think the duke simply woke one morning and decided that it was time for me to marry? That he would throw a dart at a map and pick my bride for me?"

"Didn't he?"

"Certainly. After quite a few years of warnings, deadlines and ultimatums. I wager the old man could recite the demands in his sleep. 'Do something useful with yourself, boy. Get back in your uniform and act like a man. You're a disgrace to the family.' That sort of thing."

She was silent for so long he thought he might have made a critical mistake and pushed her away. When she shook her head, he was sure of it.

He should have known better.

"Perhaps there are some benefits to not having a family after all," she said. "No one to tell me I'm a disappointment, even if I'm not."

By damn if she didn't simply take his breath away.

She tilted her head as if assessing him. "You were supposed to spend your entire life in scarlet regimentals, then?"

"Something like that. Third son and all."

"You had a better idea, though."

"No. I didn't. I just knew that I would not walk

back onto a battlefield unless Sussex was under siege."

Blast, his right hand was shaking. He dropped it to his lap, hoping she didn't see.

"When did you come to this life-altering decision?" she asked.

He tried so hard to sound off-hand. "If memory serves, I was face-down in the mud at Bayonne praying the last cannon blast had left the top of my head intact. Or it could have been a moment later when I lifted it to find that I got my wish. Except I seemed to have been the only one to have succeeded."

Now his stomach was roiling. He could smell devastation. Charred flesh and blood, thick and musty and skin-crawling. He could see Johnson's brains spattering his right arm.

"But you were at Waterloo a year later," she said, her voice softer.

He stared at that shaking arm where it lay useless in his lap and shrugged. "A brief aberrancy."

"Because your men were fighting."

"What was left of them."

And he'd delivered them up to Hougoumont. Screams. He heard screams in his sleep almost every night. He saw flames shooting up from the disintegrating thatch that covered the makeshift hospital in the great barn. He ran for nothing.

When he felt her hand curl about his, he thought he was imagining it. He hadn't felt that kind of warmth in so long. Deep, calm, gentling warmth. He looked up to see that, indeed, she had caught hold of his left hand and simply held on.

"Has the duke ever been to battle?" she asked.

He grinned. He actually grinned. "Dukes do not go into battle, my dear. Nor the eldest sons of dukes. It's why they..."

Damn. What was it about her that made him want to say too much?

But again she pulled the rug out from under him.

"Were so insistent that you did?"

He gave a jerky nod, feeling the nausea build at his own duplicity. "Exactly. Someone in the family had to make an appearance. *Noblesse oblige* and all. The funny thing is that the curate would have made a better Colonel than the Colonel did."

"Bollocks."

He kept blinking at her as if she'd changed form. "Pardon?"

She frowned. "He might have enjoyed it more. He wouldn't have cared for his men so well." When he didn't answer her, she flashed him a grin. "Don't forget. Pip adores you. She shared with the other girls every word of not only your letters but Wellington's dispatches, which she did not do with the curate's letters from Wells. I had the most execrable case of hero worship."

He wouldn't have cared for his men so well. Flint wasn't certain how he could have cared for them worse. He had begun with a company of two hundred-forty men. He had walked away from Waterloo with seventy. No. He had not taken better care of his men than anyone.

He wasn't certain how long he sat there in silence, just holding Felicity's hand. It was a burst of laughter from across the room that woke him. One of the old farmers was backslapping the other. Felicity smiled over at them as if she didn't notice how long they'd been sitting there.

"Do you think the horses are rested?" Flint asked and took back his hand, which left him feeling oddly bereft. It didn't keep him from getting to his feet.

Setting down her ale, Felicity grabbed her bonnet and followed, as if sensing his urge to flee.

They never got the chance. Even while Flint was downing the last of his own ale, he was alerted by another voice.

"There you are, Miss Felicity," he heard in broad Gloucestershire accents. Flint turned to see the pub's owner striding their way, drying his hands on a much-used towel as he smiled at Felicity.

"Why, Mr. Hawkins" she greeted him with a smile. "I did not know this was your establishment. How lovely. Your ale is the best I've tasted in the neighborhood."

His grin was delighted. "I take that as a rare compliment from a lady of quality," he said with a broad smile. He was a genial man, plump enough to betray his fondness for his own pub's food and neat enough to prove his pub was somewhere the upper classes could feel comfortable. "Did the gentleman find you?"

"Find me?" Felicity asked, looking a bit stunned. "Who?"

Mr. Brown stopped and gave Flint a little bow. "Said his name was Martin Teesdale. Said he'd brought news, and how could 'e find you? Nice chap. Young, sharpish dressed."

He suddenly had Flint's attention. "And you gave him her direction?" Flint asked, his voice sharp.

"Aye. Not a secret, is it?"

Flint turned on Felicity. "Why is he looking for you?"

She was shaking her head, her expression bemused. "I have no idea. I don't know any Teesdales."

"He is Lord Brent," Flint said, and felt his stomach drop when her eyes widened.

"Oh, Bucky," she answered with a nod and a frown. "He was a friend of the Lassiters. My last family." It didn't seem to please him. "I wonder what he wanted."

"When did he come by?" Flint asked the innkeeper.

This took some head scratching. "Yesterday morn."

"You haven't seen him since?"

Mr. Brown shook his shaggy head. "Not since he headed toward the big house."

There was only one big house in the area.

"In that case," Flint said, nudging Felicity toward the door with a hand to her back, "I'd say we should get back and see if anyone at the house has seen him. Thank you, John."

The pub owner was frowning now. "We'll keep an eye out 'ere as well, will we?"

"I'd consider it a favor," Flint said.

Before Felicity could argue, Flint had tossed her up atop Charlie.

"You haven't seen Teesdale since you left the Lassiters?" he asked, vaulting into his own saddle.

Felicity was still gathering her reins and settling her skirts. "No. Why?"

"I have." Which was when he changed direction. They weren't going back home. They were going to Gen's house, where his own houseguests had decamped.

Felicity had no idea where they were headed until they got there. She might have had a chance to ask, but once Flint heard the name Teesdale he seemed to have forgotten that she didn't know how to ride. It was all she could do to stay on Charlie as thy pounded over fields and down roads.

It might have been better that way. It gave her far less time to fret over the fact that she was about to once again meet the Siren looking as if she'd been dragged through a hedgerow backwards. She would have also wondered just what Bucky Brent wanted with her. He hadn't been a memorable man. He'd been mostly teeth and ears, his time divided between hunting with Eddie Lassiter and discussing philosophy with Eddie's father. Since Felicity had nothing to add to either pastime, they rarely crossed paths.

Except that time Eddie Lassiter had backed her against the third-floor wall demanding she tell him why she wouldn't ride with him, and Bucky had tried to intervene.

The house they approached now was a tidy Queen Anne comprised of red brick and gleaming windows. The garden was perfectly proportioned and groomed, classic geometrics in evergreen. Not one flower marred the smoothly sculpted lines of the bushes that stretched out before the house. Felicity thought the scene might have been a symphony of harmony. It struck her as sterile and over-controlled.

And she thought that before the front door

opened to reveal the siren in all her pink and blond glory, smiling as if she had just learned her lover was coming home.

Flint was off his horse and heading toward the stairs before Felicity could even complain.

"How lovely!" the siren caroled, clapping her hands. "I see you're out getting fresh air."

"Is Bucky here?" Flint demanded.

Felicity wasn't sure exactly what she was supposed to do. Were they staying? Were they to leave again if Bucky wasn't here?

Mrs. Dent-Hardy blinked, making it look like a slow dance. "Why, no. He left this morning. Why?"

Flint stopped in his tracks. "Damn."

Now both women were blinking at him.

"Bracken?" their hostess asked. "Are you disappointed you can't introduce your fiancée to him, or should I call out the militia?"

He shoved a hand though his already-mussed hair and sighed. "Sorry. I thought he had some answers for me."

After another odd pause, the Siren looked up at Felicity and smiled. "Well, if it isn't a national emergency, perhaps you could convince Miss Chambers off her horse and into the house for a bit of tea."

Felicity flushed. The flush blossomed when Flint spun around and cursed again. "Sorry."

Then without a by-your-leave, he stalked up and simply swung her off Charlie as if she were an inconvenient parcel, leaving the horses to an approaching groom. Felicity pulled away from his hands, preferring not to face the Siren while her skin shot sparks, and brushed down her skirts, as if she had just been handed down from a coach.

"How do you do, Mrs. Dent-Hardy?" she asked, hoping her smile was less strained than she felt as she dipped a curtsy. "I apologize for our precipitate arrival..."

The beautiful woman waved aside the apology and held out a hand. "Don't tell me. Flint forgot to tell you where you were bound and why."

Having no other choice, Felicity took hold of her skirts and climbed the steps toward her. "A chronic condition, I assume?"

The siren laughed. "Back to infancy. Come. Meet my remaining guests. Are you coming, Bracken, or do you prefer to scowl on my front parterre all day?"

"I'd prefer to speak to Brent."

"Well, you'll have to ride to York. He was headed for the family seat."

Finally, Flint unstuck himself and followed Felicity up the stairs.

She shouldn't have cared. But every time he drew near, her skin hummed, and that was awfully distracting. Especially for a woman who had been offered a devil's bargain, of which he was a part.

The visit was unexceptionable, a perfectly charming hour sharing dishes of tea with three very elegant creatures who seemed to go out of their way not to mention the possible engagement or the fact that Felicity had ridden over in not just a day dress, but one that looked as if she'd found it in the dust bin.

Felicity felt she comported herself well in their company. She had, after all, spent her formative years practicing just such socialization with women quite as elegant and proper. She sipped her tea, nibbled a fairy cake, and proclaimed her delight in the stories of Burns, the music of Scarlatti and the comedy of Sheridan. She mused over the weather and nodded vaguely at the mention of people she didn't know, and even the ones she did. She even made note of the fact that several of the names batted around at tea were the same that had been exchanged over dinner with Aunt Winnie. It seemed that the old woman didn't only have visitors and correspondents of her own age, but across the generations. Considering how irascible the old spinster was, Felicity was amazed at the proof that she could claim such a diverse friendship.

"Blackmail," one of the ladies insisted. A mature redhead squeezed into a younger woman's dress, she nodded sagely. "She knows everything about everyone. I wouldn't put it past her to use the information to her benefit."

Mrs. Dent-Hardy let loose her throaty laugh. "Nonsense. There is no benefit. She hasn't been seen in London in three decades. I like her."

"I do, too," Felicity said.

If she hadn't been so on edge, she might have actually enjoyed herself. But Flint was sitting right next to her, and Bucky Brent was hovering in the background. What had he wanted? Why after four months would anyone come looking for her? And how did he know where she was? It was a little late to apologize for not stepping in soon enough back at Lassiter Hall. And she was certain he had nourished no fatal attraction for her. If fatal attraction there had been, she would have expected his to be for Eddie.

So then, why?

"You must come see me without this grumpus," she heard.

Blinking, she yanked herself back from unproductive thoughts. "Of course," she told Mrs. Dent-Hardy, although the likelihood of her riding over for a coze was faint at best. Still, she smiled and followed Flint as he rose to his feet. "Thank you so much for the hospitality."

And with a general round of bobs and curtsies, she and Flint were on their way.

They were halfway home when she finally gave in to temptation and turned to Flint. "Why are you so interested in Bucky Brent?"

He turned to her, his countenance fierce. "Why did he track you down?" Felicity blinked, nonplussed. "I have no idea. I haven't even seen him for four months. Why is it important? I know you cannot be jealous. Especially of him."

"Of course not. It would be ridiculous."

Should she tell him he'd just insulted her?

"If you want to know," he said, bringing his horse to a halt in the middle of a pasture, "I don't like coincidences. His being here..."

Felicity was bringing Charlie to a halt alongside when she felt a plucking at her sleeve. Almost simultaneously there was a *crack* from behind her, and Flint jerked back.

"Go!" he yelled, pulling his horse around, its hooves leaving the ground.

"Go? Why?" Which was when she saw the blood. "My God!"

"Get going before he reloads!" he yelled. "Get Billy!"

And then he unceremoniously smacked Charlie on the rear, sending them into flight.

CHAPTER 10

FELICITY WAS GLAD THAT CHARLIE knew the way home. It was all she could do to stay aboard as he thundered over the fields. She alternated between abject terror, a prayer that there weren't any fences to jump, and a growing certainty that she shouldn't have left Flint.

He'd been shot. How could that happen? *Why?* It could be a poacher, certainly, but that *crack* had not sounded like the fowling pieces she'd heard over the years.

But what else could it be?

And then she saw the fence rise before her and forgot everything but her own survival.

"Sweet, suffering...Charlie, no!" she begged, leaning down on his neck and clutching his mane with both hands.

Evidently Charlie didn't hear her. Just as he'd been trained to do in his years on the hunt, Charlie gathered himself, his powerful hindquarters bunching, and up he sprang. Felicity thought she might have screamed. She knew she closed her eyes.

She wasn't sure how, but she leaned back as he landed, jarring her so hard she thought she might have bitten her tongue. But she didn't fall off. It was silly, but that made her laugh and pat Charlie on his sweating neck. On he ran, with her hanging on for dear life until they both clattered into the stable yard.

It seemed she didn't need to call Billy. He was running toward her before she even crunched to a halt.

"What happened?" he demanded, grabbing Charlie's bridle as the horse skidded to a halt, almost unseating Felicity for the fourth or fifth time.

"Flint...." she gasped, sliding sideways until the stablemaster caught her and set her on her feet.

Her knees buckled, and she held on to his shoulders. "Somebody shot him. On the way...to... the Siren's...house."

"The what?"

She shook her head, her breath coming in ragged gasps, her heart thundering. "Mrs. Dent-Hardy. About halfway back...in a field. He told me to... get...you..."

Billy didn't ask more, just ran into the stable. Felicity leaned against a sweating Charlie, hoping the animal wouldn't move. She wasn't sure she was going to be able to stay on her feet. She heard shouting inside the barn, and then Billy was back on one of the hacks, another groom following.

She was looking for the mounting block, when Billy pointed at her.

"Stay here," he commanded, pausing before her. "Can ya get Mrs. Windom to be ready for his lordship, then?"

She wanted to go with him, but knew even as

she clutched Charlie's reins that she'd only be in the way. She nodded and watched as Billy and the groom swept past. Then, hand to suddenly unsettled stomach, she ran for the house.

"Mrs. Windom!"

They prepared for any eventuality. Felicity had seen the blood on Flint's white shirt. She couldn't tell where it had come from but, just in case, they had hot water, lint, a bed made up, a call out for a local physician. She paced the kitchen and drove the staff mad, all sure Lord Flint would be carried back on a plank. Instead he slammed open the kitchen door and stalked in.

Felicity stared.

"We need to talk," he said without preamble and took her by the arm.

"I thought you was shot," Mrs. Windom said from the corner.

He kept walking, never taking his eyes from Felicity. "I was. I'm fine. Come along, Miss Chambers."

She felt suddenly cowed, as if she'd done something wrong. And out he dragged her through the green baize door and up two flights of stairs to the library.

"What happened?" she demanded, still feeling completely disoriented. She had expected him to come in unconscious, bleeding, dead. He looked as mad as a wet cat, but hardly grievously injured. "I saw blood."

"Yes, yes." Letting her go, he shut the door behind him. "He caught my shoulder. Third time it's been hit. Getting tiresome, actually. Sit down."

She sat. "But you should get it cared for. We're all ready..."

"Not until I straighten this out."

He took up a position between her and the massive oak desk perched in front of the even more massive windows. The sun slanted in, dust motes dancing and his hair gleaming like dark fire as he leaned over her. His eyes were gleaming even more darkly, which made Felicity shiver. That gleam was solid rage.

"What have I done?" she asked instinctively, wishing her voice didn't sound so small. Wishing her hands weren't trembling as reaction set in to his arrival.

He was safe. He was standing. She hadn't realized how important that was to her until now.

"I don't know yet," he said. Before she could respond, he spun around to the drinks table in the corner. "Brandy?"

"I don't suppose you have ale."

"I do not."

"Then brandy."

She saw that his hand was shaking as he poured, and that he was only using his left arm. Then she saw a puddle forming on the floor.

"Before we go a minute more," she said, springing to her feet, "you need to take care of that arm."

He glared at her, brandy decanter rocking gently in his hand. "I do not..."

She pointed down. He cursed and slammed the decanter down. Then, using that same arm, he downed the brandy he'd poured and slammed the glass back down as well. "It can wait."

"No," she retorted, "it cannot. Wrap it or suffer your housekeeper's wrath when her staff spends the next week trying to get blood out of the carpet."

She headed for the bell pull, but he intercepted her. "No. Here."

With an abrupt motion, he stripped off his cravat and handed it to her. Felicity accepted it and was immediately distracted by the warmth of it. The scent. Even over the metallic tang of blood, she could smell fresh air and evergreens, healthy male and something just a bit darker. Her heart started to gallop.

What a reprehensible time to have this happen. She could have withstood him without it. But it was something so personal, so vital that she felt as if she had inhaled the essence of him, and that it was bold and free and strong. Everything she wasn't. Everything she wanted.

"Well?"

He didn't look as if he had been having the same thoughts. Startling to attention, Felicity walked up to him. "Remove your jacket, please."

He did. She suffered another setback. Of course, he would be a bit sweaty, enough that the fine linen molded to his sleek frame. Blast, she was never going to get anything done if he kept enticing her. Her own hands were beginning to sweat.

He'd been shot, she reminded herself and briskly wrapped the warm linen tightly around his arm, not even bothering to demand he slip out of his shirt. He wouldn't have stood for it.

She might not have survived it.

Before she was finished, he was already moving back to the table and another pour of brandy. She followed along, tying the knot as quickly as she could.

"It is still bleeding," she all but accused, giving her work a final pat and stepping back. "You should have it stitched."

"Not now," he retorted, pouring another glass of brandy for her. "Now sit. And tell me about Teesdale."

She sat. She did not reach for the glass. She was too busy staring at him, completely nonplussed.

"Teesdale?" She gave her head a shake. "Oh, you mean Bucky. What about him? What does he have to do with you being shot? Wasn't it a poacher?"

"It was not."

She finally remembered to take the glass from his hand. "How do you know?"

He started pacing again, his own brandy glass in hand. "That was a Baker rifle you heard. Used by the 95th Rifles during the war. Excellent weapon for snipers. Not," he said, turning back on her, "poachers."

She felt her skin go clammy. "They *meant* to shoot you?"

"No," he said, his voice sharp as cut glass. "I believe they meant to shoot *you.*"

CHAPTER 11

FOR A LONG MOMENT FELICITY didn't react. Then she laughed, a sharp, high sound. "Don't be absurd."

She wasn't certain what she thought he'd do. What she hoped, maybe. Laugh, tell her it was all a joke. Nothing else would make any sense.

"Do I look as if I mean to be absurd?" he demanded. "The only reason you don't have a ball in your lungs is because you turned to talk to me."

Setting his glass down, he reached out to her. Felicity flinched, but all he did was take a fold of her sleeve between finger and thumb. She looked down.

The glass slipped out of her hand and *thunked* on the floor. She thought she might have stopped breathing. There was a ragged little hole in the material, right where she'd felt the plucking. Exactly at the level of her heart.

"That's ridiculous," was all she could think to say, her voice thin and wavery.

He let go of her and reclaimed his drink. "Tell me about Teesdale," he repeated.

She had dropped her brandy, she realized distractedly. Another stain on the carpet. She had to clean it up. She had to wipe off her dress. She bent over to retrieve the empty glass and tried to get to her feet.

"Sit down."

She sat. She stared at the empty glass in her hand, oddly intent on the prism the sun shattered through it onto the floor. Beautiful colors dancing across the softly hued carpet and to the sleek hardwood floor beyond, the dark masculine room all but disappearing into the shadows. A beautiful room. A room in which she was certain she had no place. A room that had been tidy and neat and gleaming before she arrived. She would have to ask Mrs. Windom to thank the maids. Apologize for getting brandy on the good rug. Tell her about the blood...

"Felicity."

She looked up, startled to realize she had wandered off. She took a long, shuddery breath, trying valiantly to pull her spinning thoughts back into line.

Shot. Yes. A bullet meant for her.

She shook her head. "I don't understand..."

"Neither do I," he said, setting his own glass on the desk and reaching forward to retrieve hers from her nerveless fingers. Probably afraid she'd drop it again, she thought bemusedly, maybe break it this time. "Please. Tell me what you know of Teesdale."

She looked up to see that his eyes had softened. She thought he might have been exerting a significant amount of restraint over his emotions. She couldn't understand why.

She couldn't understand any of this.

"I...only know him through the Lassiters. He

visited during school holidays. He was a friend of Eddie....young Mr. Lassiter."

She shrugged, wondering why her brain suddenly felt so foggy.

"Did you interact with him?"

"Not really. I was up in the nursery with the younger children."

Except for that one time. The time in the hallway. The time Eddie surprised her. Or had she surprised him? She had stepped out of her room to find them there in the servant's wing. He had been standing there talking to Bucky, bent close. Intent on some papers Bucky held.

Eddie had startled. He'd smiled. He'd stepped up to ask her to go riding, standing far too close. And Bucky...what had Bucky done? She remembered him interrupting only after she'd been forced to drive her knee into the part of Eddie that had obviously been doing his thinking. Offering a rueful smile at Eddie's howls of outrage and sending her on an errand to get her clear of Eddie's wrath. She remembered being ushered out of the house the next day.

"Why do you call him by his nickname?"

She shrugged, still distracted. "Everyone did. One just...did."

"Why, after all this time, would he come looking for you?" Flint asked, fully dragging her attention back. "And how would he know where you are?"

Oddly enough, Felicity's temper began to rise. "I have no idea. I told you. I rarely saw him when I worked for the Lassiters and haven't since leaving. And how are you so positive it was me? What about the line of women parading through your servants' quarters? The ones no one knows anything about?"

This time he looked straight at her. "No one asked for them by name."

Finally panic began to bubble up in her chest.

Wrong. This was wrong. It had to be.

"What else?" Flint demanded. "There has to be something else."

She was already shaking her head. "Nothing. I was the governess. I did not interact with any of the adults except to bring the children down in the evening for the requisite viewing. No one spoke to me. I ate alone. I made my report to Mrs. Lassiter once a week in her sitting room. I didn't even make up an even number at dinners, since Mrs. Lassiter's aunt lived with them."

"Then how did you know Brent visited?"

"He would be there sometimes in the evening. He and Mr. Lassiter enjoyed debating...oh, I don't know. Philosophy. Politics."

"What kind of politics?"

She shrugged, trying to remember. "I was more focused on making certain the children behaved. Mr. Lassiter was a Tory, but he always seemed unhappy with the government. Bucky did a lot of nodding. Other than that..." She shrugged again and looked up for some reassurance. "Sometimes the children would stay to hear Bucky play. He is a very talented pianist. That is all. Truly."

"That's all? You sure you're telling me everything?"

"Why wouldn't I?"

"That's what I need to find out. If you don't know why you were almost shot, then who does? And if we don't find out, then you're still in danger. Everyone on this estate is in danger."

She wanted to get up and pace, but she wasn't certain her knees would hold her. "You're bleeding again," she said, pointing to the new blood staining the linen.

"I'll live. There must be something you know, Felicity. Something that would cause someone to come after you. I want to know what it is."

Felicity looked up at him, even more off balance. "And you believe I don't? Who do you think I am?"

"I don't know, damn it!" That seemed to stop him cold. He seemed to lose color. He opened his mouth as if to speak and then shut it.

Felicity lost her breath. He was up again, shoving a hand through his hair.

"Well," she said, her voice still unforgivably weak. "At least that makes us even. I don't either."

He waved her off. "Of course, you do. You might be an orphan, but you have had twenty years to form your own character. To have your own experiences and make your own opinions."

"And yet, here we are with no answer."

He swung around again, and she was struck by the intensity of his eyes, the green eerie, like clouds presaging a summer storm.

"Who *are* you?" he demanded.

She was on her feet without realizing it. "I'm nobody!" she all but shouted back. "A school teacher. Nothing more."

He was just as suddenly standing over her. "Not nothing more. If it were nothing more, you wouldn't be in danger. If it were nothing more, I wouldn't…." He stopped abruptly, looked away. Took a breath. "I think Teesdale is the key. Your time in that house. You must know something, or you saw something you obviously don't remember."

"Something what?"

He shook his head. "I don't know. Something illegal. Something treasonous. Something.... unsavory that could be used to blackmail someone. One of the Lassiters might know."

"The Lassiters left for the Continent not long after I was let go."

That seemed to bother him even more. He nodded absently. "Could you have left with something that didn't belong to you?"

She shook her head. "No. The Lassiters were very careful about that. No thieving governesses for them."

"Why did you leave?"

"Because my portmanteaux were sitting on the front step. I decided it would do me no good to let them go without me."

That stopped him. "Why?" He'd obviously run out of patience.

She refused to look away. "Because Mrs. Lassiter had it in mind that her bastard of a governess was trying to seduce her son."

Flint went perfectly, coldly still. "Did he touch you?"

Her smile was dry. "Only once."

"What happened?"

She shrugged. "It doesn't matter."

Suddenly he was right in front of her, his hands wrapped around her arms. "Stop that!"

She froze. "What?"

He shook her. He actually shook her. "It does bloody matter. Everything matters. Don't you understand?" he demanded, his eyes suddenly dark and hot. "I'm responsible for you. I brought you here. If something happened to you..."

"If you want to be specific about it," she said, trying so hard to ease the tightness in her chest, the frantic beating of her heart. "Your father brought me here."

"But you're my responsibility! And you could have been killed today!" He kept shaking his head, as if he couldn't understand himself. "I couldn't have borne that."

And as if she hadn't been disoriented enough, suddenly Felicity found herself crushed to him, his mouth on hers, his arm around her back, his body taut as a bow.

She never had the chance to protest. She never remembered that she should. His mouth felt like fire, his arms safe harbor, his body heaven. She lost her wits, her resolve, her hesitation. Before she knew it, she found herself bowed back, her mouth open beneath his sweet assault, her tongue sparring with his. Heat flooded her, light and soul-deep satisfaction, as if her own body had to tell her that this was the place she was supposed to be, caught in this man's embrace, savoring his strength, his solid comfort, his wicked sensuality.

She was melting like warming wax, glowing, she swore, like starlight. Drinking in a life she thought had been forfeit. She was about to abandon every shred of good sense, and she didn't care. She reached up and wrapped her arms around Flint's neck to hold on.

He flinched and cursed.

Felicity jumped back, appalled that she had

forgotten his injury. "I'm so sorry…"

He stared at her as if she had slapped him. "Don't be absurd. I kissed *you*. I shouldn't have. It wasn't fair." He stepped back, his good hand raking through his hair as if it could reorder him.

"Fair?" Her hands shook as she smoothed down her own skirt. "Are you trying to seduce me?"

"No." He scowled. "I'm trying to marry you."

She didn't want her heart to skip around just because he sounded sincere. She didn't want to be confused by the warring emotions those words ignited in her chest. Life had been so simple for so long. She knew who she was, and more importantly, who she wasn't. She knew her path, and made it a point to never expect more.

If only any of this made sense. She was trying so hard to maintain her composure. And he was taking hold of her shoulders and pulling her close.

"I realized today," he said softly, "that I don't want to lose you." He rested his forehead against hers. "I think it might kill me."

CHAPTER 12

FELICITY SWORE SHE HAD FROZEN on the spot. She couldn't think. She couldn't breathe. Oh, sweet Lord, he couldn't mean it. He couldn't want her so much. *No one* wanted her so much.

For the longest moment she couldn't move, couldn't think past the fact that he had hold of her, that their foreheads met and she could feel the agitated wash of his breath against her cheek. She couldn't bear to think that he was as serious as he seemed. It would mean too much. It was too great a distance to fall.

"You plan on locking me in the larder if I refuse to stay?" she asked, trying again to be light-hearted and only sounding breathy with shock.

His smile was heartbreaking. "I hope it doesn't come to that."

He looked so serious. His expression was intense, his eyes gleaming green in the shadowy room, his hands firm around her arms. She felt his words sink deep where old dreams lingered.

The mood in the room shifted, sweetened. She couldn't breathe, suddenly, as if he were sapping her strength with just his eyes.

"We've only known each other for three days,"

she protested, her breath unforgivably weak and uncertain. "How could you possibly know?"

"Not really three days," he said, his voice very quiet. "Pip wrote me, too, you know." Could that smile get any sweeter? "She was always talking about her roommates." Felicity was holding on to control by her fingertips. She couldn't leap into his arms. She couldn't admit that meeting him in person only solidified what she had suspected since she was eight years old. That this was the man she would love her whole life. He would be the ideal by which she measured all other men. If he left her, he would leave her with no heart at all.

But she couldn't tell him. Not yet. Not before she was certain of him. Not before they both knew what was going on in this house.

Even so, she fought tears. She pulled back and stepped out of his hold, as if that would help. It didn't. It only made her feel so cold all she wanted to do was nestle right back where she belonged. Where she *wanted* to belong.

"You really do need to get your wound looked at," she said, not sounding appreciably better.

He frowned. "Felicity..."

Now she was the one shaking her head. She had almost died when she'd realized he'd been shot. She needed to step farther away from that. She needed to pull some sense out of the swirling chaos. She had to give her heart a chance to

settle. Right now, it felt as if it would stumble right out of her chest.

"I can't go this fast," she protested, and lifted her gaze to see the sudden pain in his. "Please."

"I want to marry you, Felicity."

She smiled and knew how sad she looked. "That's the problem, isn't it? I'm afraid I simply cannot go from inconvenient embarrassment to Lady Flint Bracken in less than a week. That only happens in fairy stories. And I have been nowhere near fairies my entire life."

"Will you at least think about it?" he asked so gently it hurt. "I mean, really think about it."

"It is all I've been doing."

I love you. I will love you until my dying breath. But I know better than to think I am the woman you need. Not when you walk ducal halls and I pace the corridors of second-rate schools. Not when I have no name to bring to you.

But how could she leave? He still needed her to help unravel the mysteries here. At least she could stay that long.

Instinctively she reached up to take hold of her little locket, as if to resettle herself in the world. It wasn't there.

Her locket.

"It's funny," she said with a stiff little laugh as she walked over to the bell-pull. "I just remembered something. I did bring something away from the Lassiters' with me. I didn't think of it because I didn't take what wasn't mine."

She pulled the bell for Mrs. Windom.

Flint stayed perfectly still. "What is it? How did you come by it?"

"My pupil Mary. When I left so quickly, she ran down the drive after me and gave me a trinket she said she got at a local fair. A locket."

She shook her head, the image of Mary's tear-streaked face before her. *"They shouldn't have," the*

little girl had kept saying, her hand clasped in Felicity's.
"I don't want you to forget."

There was no way Felicity could ever forget. Mary had been the first person who had needed her.

"Do you have it?" Flint asked.

Startled, Felicity looked up. "In my room. It broke when you pulled me from under the bed, remember?"

For half a minute she thought he might have smiled back at her. "Please. Go get it. I have to be sure. Quick. And Felicity."

She turned.

"We will finish this conversation. That is a promise."

She could do no more than nod and open the door.

On her way out, she asked the arriving footman to have Mrs. Windom see to Flint's wound. Then she went to retrieve the locket she prayed would mean nothing to anyone but her. After all, if it did, she might lose it.

It hadn't begun life as a locket, she admitted, as she opened the small jewelry case her friends Fiona and Mairead Ferguson had given her on their graduation. She imagined it had begun life as a watch fob, a gold-colored metal oval bearing a surprisingly well-etched lion rampant. Felicity had spent precious funds to attach it to a good chain.

Little Mary said she'd seen the trinket in a booth. Felicity smiled as she palmed the cool metal. It wasn't much, Mary had said, but it had reminded her of her dear Miss Chambers, fierce and protective. Felicity thought she would go to her grave without a finer compliment.

She paused there, her eyes misting as she thought of that little girl and wondered where she was right now. Venice? Rome? Felicity hoped so much that Mary was enjoying her adventures. She didn't want her to ever regret a thing.

If she could have, she would have handed that locket back to the little girl to remind her that she, too, was like a lion and should never forget it. But Mary had insisted that the locket was meant for Miss Felicity. After all, she'd said, the opposite side was inscribed with a large, ornate C. For Chambers.

"Don't you see?" the little girl had demanded, breathless from running to catch her. "It was always supposed to be yours."

It was. Even hours later bouncing along in a mail coach to London, when Felicity had looked more closely to see that the C was actually a G.

By the time Felicity returned to the library, the little necklace draped from her closed fist, it was to find Mrs. Windom laying out her supplies on a towel she'd spread on Flint's desk alongside his discarded cravat. He was faced away from the woman, struggling to get his shirt over his head, but Mrs. Windom didn't seem to notice that his torso was exposed up to his neck.

Felicity was sure she should feel relief at the small size of the wound on his arm, or distress at the remaining evidence of his other brushes with death, nicks and a slash that transected his flank. But truly she couldn't take her eyes off his magnificent back. Lean, taut, not an ounce of fat.

Breathtaking.

"Miss Felicity?"

She startled, realizing she'd shuddered to a stop at the door. Blinking, she saw that Mrs. Windom was gesturing to where Flint was trying to get his shirt over his head past his wounded arm.

Felicity almost flinched. The housekeeper wanted *her* to help?

Mrs. Windom glared at her. The housekeeper *did* want her to help.

Pocketing the necklace, she took a steadying breath, stepped up behind Flint and almost fainted. His back. His side. His chest. Just as lean and muscled, dusted in hair the same deep auburn as his head. Glistening a bit from the sweat of his ride. Felicity reached up to help pull his shirt over his head and deliberately took in a slow breath. She smelled horse and clean sweat and a tang of evergreen and sunlight. She felt smooth, tight skin beneath her fingers. She heard the small gasp he let out when she inadvertently touched him.

Well, maybe not so inadvertently. Her fingers tingled. They actually tingled as she carefully stripped the sleeve off the wounded arm. She found herself standing far too close and not wanting to budge. She wanted to soothe his pain and incite a fever. She wanted to wrap him in her arms and not ever let him go.

He'd been shot, and she simply didn't know how to feel about it, except that she was terrified. And not just from the danger.

And then he turned just a bit more and Felicity's breath caught in her chest. Sweet God. His other arm. With his shirt off, she could see a line of red, ropy scars that traced his muscles all the way down, almost to his wrist. Burns. She wanted to reach out to touch them, to soothe them as if they were still fresh.

What had happened to him? What had he suffered? The scars weren't that old, still looking angry and swollen. Weeks? Months? No wonder a gunshot to the arm had barely bothered him.

"Well then, young sir," Mrs. Windom scolded, rag in hand as she examined the jagged edges of the slice the bullet had taken out of Flint's arm. "It's certainly bled well for ya. Keeps infection down. Poacher, was it?"

"You know there are no poachers here, Mrs. Windom," he said through gritted teeth.

She shrugged. "Billy Burke'll sort it out."

Felicity stepped carefully away, needing a bit of room from her own reaction to the complex story of Flint Bracken's body. Before she could get out of range, Mrs. Windom caught her by the arm and handed her a pad to press against the wound

as the housekeeper threaded her needle. Felicity closed her eyes, as if that would help.

"Mrs. Windom," Flint said. "Can you ask if Lord Brent spoke to any of the staff about Miss Chambers while he was here?"

Pulling away the pad, Mrs. Windom bent to her task. "Wasn't here long enough, my lord. Never left the back salon. Where the drinks table is, isn't it?"

"Anyone else happen to mention her?"

Focused on her work, the housekeeper just shook her head. Felicity was about to make a strategic retreat when the housekeeper turned and handed her a pair of scissors. Oh, blast. Felicity hated this part. Taking in a surreptitious breath, she stepped closer. When Mrs. Windom finished the stitch, Felicity cut the thread. She was proud of herself. She didn't even shudder.

"Substitute teacher for battlefield medicine?" Flint asked.

Felicity smiled. "Little girls are more rough-and-tumble than men think."

She cut another thread, wanting all the while to ask about those burns. She tried not to notice that Flint's hands were curled in on themselves or that she could hear his teeth grind. Knowing how much this must hurt did nothing for her peace of mind. She wanted to hold his hand. She wanted to hold his head. She wanted to go back an hour and prevent this from happening at all. She wanted to go back far enough to prevent every scar on his body.

The only thing she could think to do was distract him.

"Here," she said, pulling out the locket.

She expected him to glance at it and nod. He didn't. He went suddenly still, his eyes widening a bit, his nostrils actually flaring.

Her stomach dropped. She almost pulled her hand back and ran.

"Where did you say you got this?" he demanded, reaching out to take it.

Felicity took a breath. "I told you," she said, grudgingly handing over the locket and broken chain. "My pupil. Mary Lassiter. She got it at a local fair."

"No." He didn't even look up. "She did not."

Felicity very much feared she had just lost her

most precious possession. "How do you know?"

He spared a quick glance for Mrs. Windom, who was wrapping his arm. "I'll show you when I have two hands."

Mrs. Windom didn't even look up from where she was tying off the linen bandage. "Haven't given away state secrets to the French yet, now, have I?"

Even so, with a scowl at her employer, she gathered her things and departed, her skirts swishing briskly as she walked. Flint waited until the door closed before moving. Handing the locket back to Felicity, he recovered his shirt and gingerly donned it. Felicity resented the little locket of a sudden. Without it she would have happily drunk in the play of Flint's taut muscles as he lifted his arms and slid the shirt over his head. Instead she found herself rubbing her thumb over the swirling pattern of a lion rampant and thinking of Mary.

"How do you know she didn't get it at a fair?" she asked the minute his curling auburn hair appeared through the neck of the shirt.

He pointed with one hand while settling his shirt with the other. "See the lion?"

"Yes."

He reclaimed the locket before she could object. "That particular lion is the identifying mark of a group of traitors known as—-unimaginatively enough—the Lions. Each member carries something like this to identify himself."

And little Mary had given it to her.

"Traitors how?" she asked, her voice suddenly very small.

He shrugged, still examining the locket. "Traitors the way traitors usually are. Trying to take over the throne. Well," he amended, slipping his thumbnail into the locket's opening. "Trying to put Princess Charlotte on the throne so they can control her and bring back the Golden Age of the Aristocracy."

"But we already have someone on the throne. Several someones, in fact."

The locket *snicked* open. "Indeed."

Another chill chased down Felicity's spine. She leaned over to see how he would react to what he uncovered.

"A key?" Flint asked.

Not an actual key. The engraving of a key on the inside of the open locket. Other than that, the locket was absolutely empty.

"Indeed," she echoed. "What do you think it means? I always assumed it was the key to someone's heart. I imagine you are going to say it is not."

After running his fingers over all the surfaces as if seeking an opening he hadn't expected, he snapped it shut. "What can the G be for?" he asked himself, still turning the little gold-colored trinket in his hands. "G…G." He shook his head. "Can't think of anyone among the Lions with the initial..." "You know who these people are?"

"We have an idea. You say that Bucky visited the Lassiters while you were there. Did anyone else?"

"Of course. The Lassiters were a very social couple. But I don't know anyone else's name. The only reason I know Bucky is because of his music. He would sometimes help the children perfect lessons on the pianoforte when he was there. None of the Lassiters' other friends would have been that considerate. Nor thought to be introduced to the governess." She paused, suddenly appalled. "You cannot think Bucky is a traitor."

"At this point, I can count no one out. If Mary had told you the truth about where she got this, we might have a better idea. Any of the Lassiters or their friends could just as easily be our target. Or all of them could be."

"Or she really did get it from the fair."

He was already shaking his head. "No. No little girl would be able to afford a gold locket. And no one would mistake it for anything but gold."

No one but Felicity, evidently.

"I imagine they see what they expect to," she murmured in her own defense.

His whole attention was on the locket. Felicity's was on him. She was feeling the ground slip out from under her. She had been subject to too many warring emotions in too short a time.

Suddenly his words caught up with her. "You said our," she said.

He didn't look up. "Hmmm?"

"You said *our*. We. We who?"

That got his attention. He looked up, and suddenly those sharp green eyes had somehow gone opaque. "Well…," he said, finally looking up. "The, uh, government…"

Felicity blinked, waiting for more.

"The government," she prompted when he stopped. "You serve the *government*?"

He shifted, as if anxious to flee. "In a way."

"In what way?"

She kept watching him, waiting for more. Feeling as if she should already know the answer. He kept turning the locket in his hand. She had a feeling he was in the process of inventing some outlandish answer. And then, out of the blue, she swore she could hear Pip's voice.

"Nobody can know, of course. He'd murder me if he knew I told you."

The pieces of the puzzle clicked right into place.

"Oh, my heavens," Felicity breathed. "You're a rake!"

He froze as if she'd called him a witch, but only for a second. Then his patented grin flashed. "Merely popular."

She scowled at him. "You know perfectly well what I mean. You work with Pip's brother Alex and his friends. Don't you?"

"How do you…Oh." If he weren't so in control, his shoulders would have slumped. "Pip knows."

"Well, of course Pip knows. We are speaking of Pip here. She told us when her brother Alex brought her friend Fiona back to school after she ran off. Pip was trying to convince us that we could trust Alex to get her back. Because he was a spy. A member of Drake's Rakes."

"Not a…"

She scowled. "A *spy*. Among a group of other spies who were all sons of the aristocracy. Have you done this since you left the army? Or did you do it then too?"

It was his turn to scowl. "I help when I can. I have helped on the Lion investigation. But you cannot tell anyone else."

Felicity spared him a scowl. Something still made her feel uncomfortable, but she couldn't put her finger on it. Maybe she would be able to better contemplate it later when she was in her room. Away from the very distracting presence of Lord

Flint Bracken.

In the meantime, she could protect her locket.

"You've seen it," she said, her own hand hovering over his that was closed around her necklace. "Would there be any harm in my having it back?"

She didn't want to beg, but she would.

Flint's smile was rueful. "Not yet. This has to be shared with others who might be able to recognize something important that I don't. Fortunately, a couple are in the vicinity."

She would never get it back. She didn't know how she was so certain, but her little locket was already lost. Her throat closed a moment against the sharp sting of tears, but she nodded and deliberately took a step back.

"I'll take very good care of it, Felicity," he said, his voice soft.

She nodded again and backed a few more steps away. "I'll, uh, just..." She gave her hand a little wave. "You need to change, don't you?"

And before he could say another word, she turned and walked out, shutting the door behind her, her emotions in more of a turmoil than she could ever remember. Without thinking, she headed down toward the servants' stairs and the kitchen. Cook looked up in surprise as Felicity hurried past, but she couldn't stop.

"Your dress, Miss…."

She just needed some air. Some space. She needed to sit among a few flowers that didn't want anything from her but to bloom. To scent the air. They didn't even mind if she got a bit sniffly. Ridiculous thing to get weepy over, an empty locket. Rather maudlin, actually. Poor little orphan girl losing her most precious possession, which wasn't precious at all, except to spies. And her.

Her escape to the garden was probably a mistake. Autumn seemed to have taken hold while she wasn't watching. Low, thick clouds rolled across the sky, herded along by a chilly snapping breeze that managed to sneak right up under skirts and chill the skin. The flowers were all but gone. She should have known. The bench she sought out sat in isolated splendor in a naked walled garden that already slept. No blooms. No pretty color or comforting scents to remind her that no matter which way she turned after this moment there would still be spring.

And the bench was cold.

She wasn't certain how long she sat there, her hands clasped in her lap, her head down, thinking nothing. Not how much import she had put on a silly little necklace, not how much she was beginning to put on a handsome man. Not what would happen next or what price she would pay. She just sat, the silence gathering like a clean wall between past and future. Autumn and spring. Experience and possibility or pain. Undoubtedly pain, if past experience counted for anything.

"Miss Chambers! Oh, thank heavens!" she heard.

She snapped to attention, her head up, her mouth open to call out.

"No," Bucky begged, hand up, face crumpled in distress.

Looking at him now, who could think he was a traitor? He crept around the garden wall like a dog expecting to be whipped, his plump young face creased in distress, his usually perfectly styled

Brutus cut gone wild.

"Did you shoot at me, Bucky?" she demanded.

"No!" He stepped closer so that she noticed that his attire was just as crumpled as his expression. If there was one thing Bucky was proud of, it was his sartorial elegance. If his current look was any indication, he was in terrible distress.

"Please," he begged. "You must have my watch fob. Mary gave it to you, didn't she? I need it back. You need to give the code to me and the list before both of us are murdered. They won't take no for an answer."

Felicity found herself shaking her head. "I don't have it, Bucky. Would you like to come in and talk to Lord Flint?"

His color went ashen. "Are you mad? They'll kill me for sure. As it is, I'll be off for…well, away anyway. But I need to get them the list before I go, or I will be hunted down."

"Bucky, you cannot mean to help overthrow the throne."

"Of course not," he snapped. "It was a game. A…well…just an exercise. How could I know he meant it?"

"He who?"

But he was shaking his head and looking around, even though they were in a walled garden. "Can't you get it for me? If not the locket. The list."

"List?" She echoed. "I have no list."

"Of course, you do. I gave it to you myself."

"No, you didn't, Bucky. I only brought along what was absolutely mine. I don't have anything else."

She honestly thought he was going to weep.

"Then I have to go. Be careful. They think you have it. They will continue to be after you."

"They who? Who shot at me, Bucky?"

"Reed. Just tell Bracken it was Reed. He'll know. Be careful. Reed knows the ins and outs of this place. He visits Lady Winifred because of John Harvester. Bracken will understand. And Miss Chambers? If you do find that list…destroy it. It would be better than letting it get into their hands, truly. Tell Bracken it's all I can do."

And before she could think of anything else to say to keep him there, he ran out of the garden. Within a minute, she heard hoofbeats thunder off toward the road.

She sat back down, the air completely taken out of her.

Bucky. She had to tell Flint. She had to get out of this garden, no longer a safe haven, if Bucky was right. But if he was right, nowhere was a safe haven.

She rose to her feet, her knees a bit shaky, and returned through the kitchen door.

"Miss!" the cook protested as she passed. "Your dress! It must be sponged."

Felicity just nodded and kept walking. *List.* Bucky thought she had a list. And a code. She'd have to think about that. After she told Flint.

But when she reached the study, Flint was gone. He and the locket had disappeared along with his horse, and no one could say when he'd be back.

"Did Mr. Burke go too?" she asked Higgins when she met him in the hall.

"Yes, Miss."

She nodded absently. "I know that you take the

safety of this house seriously, Higgins."

"His lordship has increased the security," he assured her, straightening. "We're all tucked in like badgers in a sett."

"Of course. Do you know a person named Reed? I understand he comes to visit Lady Winifred."

He frowned. "Mr. Francis? Of course."

"Well, if you see Lord Flint, warn him that Mr. Reed is the one who shot at me."

Higgins stiffened as if she'd accused him. "Mr. *Francis?* Oh no, Miss. That couldn't be. Why, Mr. Francis is here all the time visiting Lady Winifred. He wouldn't..."

Felicity faced him down. "He did, Higgins. There is also something about a John Harvester. Do you know him?"

"He used to visit as well. Served with Lord Flint."

Used to. Past tense. At least not a current threat.

"Please secure Mr. Reed if he appears. It will be up to Lord Flint what do to with him. And if you would let me know when Lord Flint gets back..."

She didn't wait for his answer, just turned to the stairs and her room. She needed to change into her one other dress. Cook was right. This one needed to be sponged. There was blood on it. Flint's blood. Flint, who was a spy. Flint who had just ridden right back out as if the person who had shot him no longer posed a threat.

The person who was not Bucky, but Reed, who evidently felt right at home at Hedgehog Haven because he visited Aunt Winnie.

Maybe Flint would understand. She certainly didn't.

"Miss," the maid said as Felicity passed. "Miss

St. Clair was hoping to see you when you have a minute. Something about the larder."

Felicity almost smiled. Aunt Winnie was never that polite. "In a little bit, Sukie."

Should she say something to Aunt Winnie? She wondered heading on past. No. Not until she spoke to Flint. Reed wouldn't get past Higgins 'til then.

Deciding she'd had quite enough, she escaped into her room. She closed the door behind her and slipped out of her dress. Then, feeling as if she didn't have an ounce more energy left in her, she stretched out on her bed and closed her eyes.

And promptly remembered quite clearly where the list was.

CHAPTER 13

SHE SHOULD HAVE TOLD HIM right away. After all, this was treason they were dealing with. Lives were at risk. Very important lives. But Felicity decided that since Flint failed to present himself at dinner, she had the right to escape his aunt's rambling complaints afterwards to hole up in her room with her music.

Specifically, the music sheets she thought she had accidentally included from one of her students. When she had realized what it was Bucky was so desperate to retrieve, she'd thrown on her clean dress and run right down to the music room, where her sheet music sat in the hinged bench. Mozart and Bach and Purcell and...Bucky.

She should have taken a closer look at the piece before, she thought, pulling it out of the pile. She would have noticed the almost Gregorian chantlike repetition of notes which, when played, made no melodic sense. She would have remembered that it was sheet music Bucky had pushed into her hand that last day and asked her to take down to the music room to get her away from Eddie Lassiter. Evidently when the staff had piled all her belongings together to get her out of the house the next day, they had not separated out her music from anyone else's.

The piece was no more than two pages written in the key of B, beginning with the line:

d d d c f f f | f f g f f e | a a a f f f g b b a a a | b b b a d d d e e e a a a g g

She had to assume this was the list Bucky had wanted. Words, she thought. Places? Names? Dates? She rubbed at the bridge of her nose, a habit she'd developed when working out mathematical problems. She wished her friends Fiona and Mairead Ferguson were here. They would have known how to go about this in a minute. But then, the two of them were geniuses. Even in school they had corresponded with some of the greatest mathematical and astronomical names in the kingdom. In Europe, for that matter. They used to construct their own personal codes and challenge their fellow students to solve them. Then they had all communicated that way to avoid discovery by their headmistress, the dreaded Miss Chase. Felicity had been one of their most enthusiastic students.

Patterns, they'd said. Always look for patterns. The pattern she saw here was repeated notes, with half rests separating some, whole rests others. Different words? Different letters? The whole rest separated the word, she thought. The half rest might have divided multiples of the same notes into separate letters.

She nodded to herself. Suddenly feeling a little less lost, she pulled a sheet of foolscap from the little red lacquer escritoire that sat beneath her window. Finally, something that felt familiar.

If the notes stood for letters, there couldn't be

a one-to-one substitution. There simply weren't enough letters in music. Only A to G. Which meant the rest would have to simply be a repetition of the first seven.

She laid out a grid.

A B C D E F G
H I J K L M N
O P Q R S T U
V X Y Z

If she was right, then the translation would be as easy as using that top line in repetition to identify other letters. O would be AAA. N would be GG. Working off her grid, she worked through the first page, separating the letters into words according to the rests.

As she suspected, it wasn't enough. She sat back and considered. Her repeated letters, which should have translated into something recognizable, didn't.

dddcfff | ffgfff became RQTMUT

dddd | gaagg became ZUUHGG

Hmm, she thought, considering her patterns. *What was it Bucky had said? He needed the list. And he needed the locket.*

The locket.

Suddenly she was grinning. Of course. Every code needed a key, and he'd been looking for it. And if the locket meant anything, the key was G. As in the musical key of G.

But how did it fit? The key signature of the music was in B, but all transposing it to G would do would be to remove two sharps. It wouldn't change the letters.

B. G.

B, C, D, E, F, G. Five steps. Could it be that simple?

Just transpose the letters up five steps?

She shook her head. Bless poor Bucky. He was a good musician. He was a far less proficient code maker. She bent back to her work with a will. But instead of translating the notes as she had, she raised the notes by five. An A became an F. B became G. She transposed again.

Nothing.

It should have fit. The key was G. It had to be. She sat for a moment and looked at her grid. Then she laid her letters out on a treble clef, as if teaching music. That was when she saw that she had another option. G was five steps above B. It was also two steps *below* B. Two steps down.

And there it was.

dddcfff | ffgfff became PARKER.

 ddddg | gaagg became WEEMS.

She smiled to herself, a hunter spotting the prey peeking through the brush. And for a moment, she was back in school, trying to smother her giggles so the headmistress wouldn't know what she and the other girls were up after lights out in order to outwit the staff.

By the time she finished, the hour was late. She thought of sneaking down to Flint's room to share her results, but decided against it. They were safe in this lovely old house for the moment. And for just a few more hours, she would like to pretend that the last name she had translated had not been Lassiter. That Mary would grow up in peace and safety.

Looking down at the fourteen names she had

translated, some of which belonged to girls she had shared classrooms with, she considered that just perhaps it was a good thing she had no name but the one she had created for herself. She wouldn't have to face a betrayal from her own family.

Tucking her papers under her pillow, she changed into her threadbare old cotton night rail and blew out the candles. She was exhausted and knew she would have to rise in just a few hours, but she still found sleep long in coming. She couldn't stop thinking of the reception she would get from Flint when she showed him her work.

Much to Felicity's chagrin, she overslept. The first she knew, Sukie was throwing back the curtains, and the delicious aroma of chocolate tickled her nose. She was in the process of stretching when she realized that the sunlight was far too bright.

"Oh, no." Throwing back the covers, she scrambled out of bed. "What time is it, Sukie?"

"Going on ten, ma'am. You didn't ask me to wake you at a specific time, and you seemed to be sleepin' so sound."

Quickly finishing her ablutions, Felicity picked up the dress Sukie had laid out for her. "Is Lord Flint up and about?"

Sukie rolled her eyes. "Oh, laws, yes, Miss. He be closeted in with the duke hisself, what came down first thing."

Felicity stopped, her dress still up around her ears. "The duke?"

"Oh, yes, Miss. I believe they're havin' words about the girls come through here."

Felicity went back into motion. "I imagine they are."

For just a moment she contemplated the thought that today might be the day she formally accepted Flint. Not because her feelings for him had changed. Because her feelings for herself had. Until this moment, she could have named nothing of value she would be bringing to her marriage. Oh, she could organize a household, but Flint didn't seem all that consumed by a domestic agenda. She could play and teach music, but so could any girl in his circle.

But now she could bring a skill those girls did not possess—well, unless they went to boarding school with the Ferguson twins, anyway. She could break codes. Surely that would be an aid to a man helping the government uncover plots. After all, she already had information for him. Information he couldn't have obtained without her.

By the time Sukie had pinned her mistress's hair into a simple knot, Felicity was humming. She actually felt a bit breathless, skittery.

Excitement. She couldn't remember ever flirting with such an emotion. Anticipation. Just a wee bit of fear. After all, this could change everything.

Oh, lord, she thought, pressing a hand to her suddenly unsettled stomach. I'm to be married. Who would ever have thought?

"There you go, Miss. You look a right treat, you ask me."

Felicity bounded to her feet and gave her maid a hug. "Thank you, Sukie. You're a wonder."

The girl blushed. "Aw, now, don't go bein' silly."

Felicity laughed and trotted over to retrieve her

annotated sheet music and notes from beneath the pillow. A bit crinkled now, but still perfectly clear. Still a list of prominent British families who might just possibly be traitors, including poor Bucky.

All right, perhaps she felt a bit more fear. After all, whoever 'they' were, they knew she had this. They had to know she would share it if she realized what she had. Thank heavens she was about to marry into a very prominent family.

"Miss," Sukie interrupted her, hand out. "You might want this. There's a chill in the air."

Felicity caught hold of her brown knitted shawl and swept out the door.

Felicity saw Higgins closing the door of the Green Salon as she reached the bottom of the staircase. When he caught sight of her he approached, his posture so stiff she thought he might crack, his attire flawless, his sparse hair slicked down without a strand displaced. Higgins was usually quite tidy. This was excessive.

"The duke is here, is he?" she asked with a smile.

He did not smile back. "He is indeed, Miss. Lord Flint is speaking with him in the library."

"About our house guests?"

He cast a quick look around, as if afraid the duke would sneak up on him. "One would assume. Would you like some breakfast? I can have Cook send something up."

"Thank you no, Higgins. I am far too restless. I shall be quite well."

Oddly enough, this seemed to stiffen the butler even more. He cast a look over his shoulder and took a breath, as if coming to some decision. "In that case, Miss, may I suggest you wait in the Green

Parlor next door to the library. I will let Lord Flint know you wait."

If she hadn't thought Higgins would perish of mortification, Felicity would have kissed his cheek. "Thank you. I shall do exactly that. We haven't heard from Mr. Reed, I presume?"

Higgins frowned. "You're certain about that, Miss? I cannot imagine Mr. Reed causing harm. Why he was just here last week."

Felicity nodded. "I'm afraid so. The warning was quite clear."

And his name was on the list.

He sighed. "Well, nothing is out of the ordinary here."

"Except for the duke."

He gave her a solemn nod. "Except for the duke."

She would have preferred to wander the garden where she could have turned her face up to the sun and basked like a cat. But after Bucky's warning the night before, she didn't feel quite so capricious. The Green Parlor would do quite well with its emerald silk-papered walls and comfortable cream-colored settees. She should have brought a book, of course, especially since the library was currently occupied. Sitting and waiting were not her best talents.

It turned out, though, she neither sat nor waited. The minute she entered the salon she heard voices. She looked around, but she was the only one in the room. Then she saw that the door into the next room was cracked ever so slightly.

She turned back to check with Higgins, but the butler had silently closed the parlor door behind her. The scapegrace, she thought with a grin. He had been eavesdropping on his master's conversation with the duke.

She knew she shouldn't sink so low. She swore she could withstand temptation and take herself to the other side of the room. She would quietly sit and go over the music crumpled in her hands, the list she'd pulled from the notes.

Wrapping the shawl tightly around her shoulders, she quietly stepped across the pink and green Aubusson carpet toward the settee. Now that she had made her mind up that marriage to Flint would benefit both of them, she wanted to get the resolution over with. She wanted him to know. She wanted to see how he received her decision.

She wanted to see his eyes light when he realized what she offered. Clutching the sheets more closely, she smoothed her skirt as she prepared to sit and wait.

"You're certain she isn't pulling the wool over?"

Felicity heard the clipped baritone voice and stopped. The duke. It must be. His tones were even plummier than his son's, and his voice rang with command. Felicity literally held her breath.

"I am," Flint answered easily.

"Even though she was carrying the fob."

That stopped even her breathing. Felicity froze, the sheet music crinkling in her suddenly clenched hands.

"I believe her story," Flint answered.

"The search of her things turned up nothing?"

"Nothing more than the possessions of an impecunious music teacher, just as she said."

"And you used your considerable talents on her to make absolutely sure."

There was a long pause. Felicity didn't breathe.

"Of course, I did."

She felt as if she'd been kicked.

There was a rather indelicate snort. "Well, your… *skills* have never failed you before. I admit I hoped she was as guilty as the rest of them. It would have made it easier all round."

"For you, maybe."

"It would have saved us time."

"Those women you've been foisting on my household weren't any help?"

"They were, actually. Housemaids, mostly, recruited by Diccan Hilliard. But they didn't have the same access of Miss…Chambers? Is that what she calls herself?"

"Yes. Why? Do you know something she doesn't?"

"I know quite a few somethings most people don't. The pertinent fact, though, is that we can send her back to that school of hers."

There was a small pause. "I'm to break it to her gently?"

"Well, don't tell her that you *never* meant to marry her. Just tell her that I changed my mind."

Never? He had never meant to marry her? Felicity thought she might vomit right onto the carpet.

"And I get the house," she heard him say.

"I made a promise, did I not?"

Felicity stood there in the shadows just beyond the door feeling sicker by the minute. She wanted to run. She wanted to scream. She looked down at the freehand score she held, the tune embedded in her brain where she knew it would remain until she forgot her own name.

It would be so easy to threaten them with it. Hold it hostage until they set her up someplace she could be comfortable. And alone. It sounded good, suddenly, living by herself somewhere she couldn't again be so bitterly disappointed.

Sadly, she had too many scruples. And Flint was right. She was a dreadful liar. There was only one thing to do.

She didn't even bother to knock. She just pulled the door all the way open and walked in, her heels clacking against the hardwood floor. Still gleaming, she thought absently as she crossed the room. It was better to think about than the sick realization in Flint's eyes as he jumped to his feet.

"It would have been much easier just to ask," she said, keeping a dreadful control over her voice as she lifted her gaze to his. "But I imagine the games are more fun."

"Felicity..."

At least his voice sounded strained. A better actor than she, obviously. She didn't give him a chance to continue. Deliberately turning from him, she faced the duke, who didn't even bother to look chagrined. "I had heard you like to play with people's lives. Be careful one of them doesn't play back." The duke sat behind Flint's desk, a silver-haired near twin to his son.

Well, Felicity thought inconsequentially, *at least Flint had never had to question* his *parentage.*

The duke rose slowly to his feet. His brow gathered. "You had better not be threatening me, young lady. The fate of the nation is at risk."

She gave him a smile that seemed to take all her energy. "I imagine as an excuse that will do for you. Still, some people won't be as understanding as I."

"However?" he retorted.

"However, nothing. I do not play games, Your Grace. Although I will make this one demand. Since you saw fit to blithely interfere with my life, you may now restore it. In exchange for these papers which I believe are what you were looking for, you may secure me my old position so I never have to cross your path again. Have we an agreement?"

"I can simply take them."

She lifted an eyebrow. Evidently disdain was all it took to learn a new skill.

Flint answered for her. "You would never sully your hands," he told his father. "And I can't think of anyone here who would help. They like her better than they like you."

The duke never looked toward his son. "I would have your help, or I would take your house back," he told him anyway.

"And lose any reputation you have left as a gentleman," Flint retorted. "I would make certain of it. Right after I burned the house to the ground."

The duke actually looked surprised. For a moment, there was silence. Then he deliberately turned back to Felicity. "You were always to be accepted back to your little school, Miss...er, Chambers. My best wishes for your future endeavors."

He held out his hand. Without another word, Felicity dropped the papers into them and turned to leave. Behind her, the duke snorted rather indelicately. "It seems all that money spent on Miss Chase's Academy was a waste after all."

She had just been about to leave. With those

words, though, her previous disinterest in her background shattered. She stopped and turned.

"So, you *do* know why I was sent there."

He lifted an imperious eyebrow that almost made Felicity laugh out loud. At least she finally knew where Flint had learned that trick. "Of course, I know."

"Then you won't mind telling me."

"Why should I?"

She shrugged. "Why not? Lady Winnifred said something about the school, that girls were sent there for a reason. What reason?"

"Safety. Men in power are targets of blackmail and extortion. Their children make them vulnerable."

She nodded, her chest growing painfully tight. "Especially bastard children, I imagine. I was not the only one there."

He didn't even bother to nod.

She did. "I shouldn't be surprised, I suppose, that people like you were more concerned for grown men than their inconvenient girl children."

He got ruddy. "That wasn't my fault..."

"I'm sure. So, my father was a man of...power?"

"I thought you didn't want to know."

She caught her breath, swinging on Flint, who stood by looking not nearly outraged enough. "You *told* him?"

He lifted his hands in a helpless gesture. "I did not."

"Your headmistress did," the duke informed her. "You and my niece evidently broke in to look at files."

"I see. Did Miss Chase get paid to spy on us?"

"No. Miss Schroeder did."

Another blow to the stomach. Miss Schroeder, who had swooped in to save all the girls from the abuses of Miss Chase. Miss Schroeder, whom they thought they could all trust. Of course she must have worked for this man. Of course she would have passed on the big and little secrets she'd learned over the years. And yet, it felt like a worse betrayal than Flint's. Felicity had never quite trusted Flint. He had always seemed too good to be true. She had trusted Miss Schroeder.

Really, she should have known better.

"Oddly enough," she said without looking at Flint, "I seem to have changed my mind. Why was I given a place at Last Chance Academy?"

The duke kept his silence.

Flint turned on him. "You will tell her, or I'll have this place burned down with you still in it," he snapped.

The duke stiffened. "How dare..."

"How dare *you*, sir? Have you become so lost in your own consequence that you no longer consider human cost? Tell. Her."

The older man shot his son a glare that Felicity was certain had intimidated legions. Flint didn't so much as blink.

Finally, the duke turned back to Felicity. "Because your father was a high-ranking diplomat connected to the house of Bracken. My sister-in-law's step-brother."

Felicity was still trying to weave through all of Pip's family stories to find a connection when Flint burst out laughing. "Good God. Uncle Andrew is her father?!"

She turned on him. "You mean Randy Uncle

Andy?" she retorted much too loudly, stunned.

The duke actually flinched. "That is the Marquess of Melborne, young lady."

Felicity shook her head, rather enjoying the duke's evident discomfort. Although why he should be disconcerted, she didn't know. According to Pip, he had been the one to send Pip's cousins and brothers out to Randy Uncle Andy for training in the 'manly' arts.

That thought brought its inevitable conclusion. "Good God. Pip *is* my cousin." She swung around on Flint. "*You're* my cousin. Did you know?"

The glare he was directing at his father was positively deadly. "Of course not. How could I? And that's *step*-cousin."

She had a family. She had Pip after all. She had... No, there was no benefit to claiming the men in this room.

"And my mother?" she asked.

"Died in childbirth," the duke said. "You cannot threaten her."

Felicity felt that blow like a slap across the face. Worse was Flint's responding silence.

"You are perfectly correct, of course," she said, keeping rigid control of her emotions. "What could my existence possibly be but a threat? Thank you for reminding me. From what I've heard Uncle Andy is also gone. No chance of blackmail there, either, is there? Now, if you don't mind, I shall be gone."

"You won't explain this to us?" The duke asked, lifting the papers.

"You seem an intelligent sort," she said without stopping. "I am certain you'll figure it out." She did stop then, mere steps from the door, but refused to face them. "Oh, I should probably check, just to be sure. Did you get the message about that person named Reed?"

"We did," the duke said. "How did you get it if you weren't involved?"

"Bucky stopped by. He did not shoot at me. Reed did. Bucky said it had something to do with John Harvester, whoever he is." She heard Flint suck in a startled breath, but didn't think she had the strength left to learn more. "Bucky did give me the key to decoding the list. You won't find him for more, though. He's gone."

The key. She truly had lost her locket. All she could do was shake her head and start walking again.

"Felicity, listen to me," Flint protested, his hand out as well.

"No," she said, her focus on the door she needed to get through. "Not again. Never again. And if you follow me, I swear on my grandmother's grave I will knee you in the cods."

Felicity threw the door open to find Higgins standing just on the other side. "Word has been sent, Miss," he said gravely. "Sukie will accompany you. She is packing your things."

"Were you listening, Higgins?" the duke demanded.

"Yes, Your Grace," the butler said. "My resignation is on the desk in my quarters."

And he turned to hold onto Felicity's arm as she walked out.

Which was the moment Felicity finally broke. She couldn't say a word. But when she nodded up at the sorrowful man, there were tears streaming down her cheeks. Even so, she kept walking right out of Flint's life and back into her own.

CHAPTER 14

FLINT ONLY WAITED FOR THE door to close behind Felicity to turn on his father.

"Do not move from this room," he said. "I shall be right back." "Where do you think you're going?" the duke demanded.

"To protect the only thing I care about."

He absently waved a hand. "I said you had the house."

Flint just shook his head. "She's right. You truly have lost any humanity that might remain."

"Come back here and finish this," the duke snapped.

Flint didn't so much as turn around. "Go to hell, sir. Or stay here until I get back. I don't much care."

By the time Flint reached her, Felicity was halfway up the great staircase, Higgins just behind her.

"Felicity," he called.

She ignored him.

"Higgins," he growled striding after them, "stop."

But astonishingly, Higgins didn't even pause.

Flint reached the bottom of the stairs. "Higgins. She is in danger. Do you want her death on your conscience?"

That brought everyone to a stop halfway up the staircase. Higgins looked over his shoulder. Felicity did not. Flint saw a shudder go through her and very much feared he was going to see tears if she turned. He wasn't so certain he could withstand that at that moment. He wished like hell she had not heard that conversation just now.

"Please, Felicity," he said. "We have no idea where Reed is. If you go outside, you could walk right into his hands. You are no longer safe. No matter how you feel about me, please don't leave the house."

"You truly think it is possible of Mister Francis?" Higgins asked.

Flint sighed. "I simply don't know anymore, Higgins. But I cannot take the chance. You know that."

A step above Higgins, Felicity seemed to shrink a bit. She didn't bother to turn around.

"All right," she said, "I'll stay." Then she turned to pat Higgins's hand. "Now go downstairs and rip up that resignation. I couldn't bear you leaving on my account."

Flint saw his butler turn to her and was astonished to see tears in the old man's eyes. "We'll find him, Miss," he said. "Don't you worry. Billy Burke will never let you be hurt."

She actually stretched up on her toes and kissed the butler's cheek. "I know," she said.

"Billy Burke?" Flint echoed, having had just about enough. "Don't be absurd. *I* won't let you be hurt. It's why I'm asking you to stay."

She nodded without facing him. "Thank you." Her voice was as flat as Sussex.

He wanted to hit something. Why had she been listening? He could have prevented this.

"Felicity, I need to talk to you."

"Maybe later," she said in a way that sounded like 'not ever.'

And damn it all if he didn't just stand there like a rock as she climbed the rest of the way up and disappeared into the shadows. He should run after her. He should drag her into his room so she had to listen to him even if she did, as she threatened to do, knee him in the cods.

He should give her a little time before approaching her. Let her calm down. Be sensible. It would give him a chance to stanch his own bleeding. His chest ached harder than if he'd been stabbed.

"You're not leaving, I take it, Higgins," he said instead.

The butler had turned back down the stairs and was headed for the green baize door at the back of the great hall. "She needs protecting, now, doesn't she, m'lord?"

Flint would deal with him later as well. For now, he needed to get back in and settle some things with his father.

He was waiting inside her sitting room when she opened the door.

"Oh, for the love of Heaven," Felicity found herself snapping.

"Shut the door." He was pointing a gun at her.

A middle-aged man in his best Weston who looked as disheveled as Bucky. A little plump, squinting as if he were near-sighted, not too steady a gun-hand.

Well, Felicity had just about had enough.

"Mr. Reed, I presume," she said, stepping farther into the room without closing the door behind her. "Unless you're Mr. Harvester."

She might as well have kicked him by his expression. "John is dead. I said shut the door."

"And turn away from that gun? I don't think so. Should I assume Bucky told you how to find me?"

Please don't tell me one of the staff told you, she thought, knowing she would not be able to tolerate one more betrayal.

"No. I've known for a while now. Dent is safe. He's gone."

"You should be, too. You have nothing left here to fight for. The duke already has your name."

He seemed to deflate. "I must have that list. You know where it is."

She felt oddly detached, as if she were playing a scene on some stage. None of it seemed real. She had spent all her credulity on a man who didn't want her. Nothing else much mattered right now.

"I know there is a list. Bucky told me. And I told him that I took nothing with me from the Lassiters' that wasn't mine."

"But you have the key!"

She nodded, keeping as perfectly still as she could. She felt so numb. It didn't mean she wanted to be dead, and that gun was just a bit too unsteady and pointing directly at her chest. And the man holding it was sweating.

"I did," she said. "I gave it to the duke. But unless there is some secret compartment no one knows of, the only thing engraved in the gold is a key, a lion, and the letter G."

He blinked a few times. "What does *that* mean?"

She shrugged. "I'm sure I don't know. Please. Leave the way you got in. You have a chance to get away before you're found. You can't shoot me, you know. The noise would bring the entire staff up here before you could make it to the window."

He just stood there. Felicity didn't move. The numbness was wearing off. She was very much afraid she was going to start trembling any moment. She might have just been rejected, humiliated, demeaned and deserted, but she wasn't dead. She didn't think she wanted to be. Not at all.

Lord, did that mean she would survive Flint Bracken intact?

Not intact. Battered and broken and heartsick, cracked like a porcelain vase.

"Well?"

He lifted the gun.

It took Flint a half hour to extricate himself from the duke. It shouldn't have. After all, he had discovered more information than the duke had anticipated. They now had the names of twenty-five people involved with the Lions—some they had suspected, some they had not. He noted that the Lassiters were the last name on the list. Poor Felicity. She had loved that little girl.

"You don't need the locket anymore," he told his father, picking it up off the desk. "I'll return it."

His father was a second too late to retrieve it from him. "Don't be daft, boy. That is evidence."

"I'll make a copy. This one goes back to its

owner."

Which was some of the business he had to attend to. Leaving his father sputtering like a landed carp, Flint took the time to freshen up, not even bothering to call his valet. Then he broke into his own safe to retrieve something his grandmother had tucked away there five or so years before, which he thought would go very well with the locket. With both in hand, he took the front stairs two at a time until he reached the second floor.

It didn't occur to him that the hallways were suspiciously empty of staff, or that the house seemed unnaturally silent, as if it had been deserted. He was too focused on the doorway to the Chinese bedroom.

Giving his jacket a tug, he knocked.

And waited.

He knocked again. He waited again.

He never considered waiting any longer. He had asked Felicity to stay here, and she wasn't answering. And they hadn't found Francis Reed. He turned the knob and pushed.

The door opened easily in his hand, but the sitting room was empty

"Felicity?"

Nothing. He walked on through. Her room was made up, the tables cleared of any personal effects. He walked into the dressing room, anticipation curdling into dread.

It was just as empty—no people, no clothing, no Felicity. There wasn't so much as a dropped hairpin on the floor. The space looked as if it had been uninhabited for months.

He backed out much faster than he'd come in.

"Higgins!"

His voice echoed down the stairs and back.

"H-i-i-i-i-i-g-g-g-g-g-i-i-i-in-s!!!!!!"

He made it to the staircase before he heard the running feet.

"Milord!" Higgins appeared on the run from the west wing. "You'll want to come with me, Milord."

"Where?" he demanded, already moving. "And why? Do you know where Miss Chambers is?"

"I do."

Higgins turned back the way he came, towards Flint's own room. He didn't stop there, though. Flint found himself standing in front of Aunt Winnie's suite as Higgins tapped on the door.

"Higgins, what in the name of..."

But Higgins opened the door, and Flint found himself stumbling to a halt, the little box and chain in his hand falling to the floor.

They were all arrayed across Winnie's rickety, camphor-scented furniture. Aunt Winnie and Miss Chase shared the pea-green brocade settee, pale, wide-eyed, Miss Chase holding Winnie's hand. A preternaturally calm Felicity was perched on an old-gold Louis Quince chair facing Francis Reed on the other Louis Quince, a gun in his hand, as if that made any sense.

At least the gun wasn't pointed at Felicity. It was pointed at Reed's own head.

"Hello, Flint," Felicity said with a quiet smile. "Won't you join us? I think Mr. Reed needs to speak with you."

"You're all right?" he asked her, stepping inside.

"I am fine." She didn't take her gaze from Reed, but she smiled. Flint wondered if anybody else

MISS FELICITY'S DILEMMA   183

could see how thin that smile was.

Flint wanted to howl. He wanted to dive into Reed and knock him to the ground. He stood perfectly still.

"Francis?"

Reed turned to him, tears streaming down his cheeks. "I'm sorry, Bracken."

Flint smiled back. "I know, Francis. But what you're about to do won't help anyone. Certainly not Melinda or John."

If it was possible, Reed looked even more broken. "It's better that she never knew."

"They've blackmailed you, then?"

There was a very small nod, Reed's eyes closing.

"Attend me, Francis," Flint snapped, unwilling to lose this man.

At least Reed opened his eyes again, his expression a rueful acknowledgement of the automatic response to a superior officer's command.

"I've been trying to tell Mr. Reed that you would find a way to protect him," Felicity said. "You were, after all, his commanding officer and are the son of a duke. That should count for something, shouldn't it?"

She smiled at the rumpled, weary, trembling Reed as if they were old friends.

Reed did not smile back.

"Of course, I will," Flint promised. "It's the least I can do when Francis restrains himself from forever traumatizing my aunt by blowing his brains all over her salon wall."

Felicity glared. Aunt Winnie gasped. Thank God, Francis didn't.

"Please, Francis," Flint said, his heart stuttering

in his chest. "This isn't the way. You know it. If you do this, we'll never have a chance to find a way to save you. Or, for that matter, to save the king and regent. You know how deadly serious the Lions are. So serious they would ruin far more lives than yours. They would ruin Melinda's. She would suffer for your secret."

Still, Francis didn't move.

And then, Felicity did, making Flint's heart stumble.

"Who is Melinda, Mr. Reed?" she asked, leaning forward to lay a hand on his knee. "Is she your wife?"

His face crumpled even more. "My daughter."

"Melinda Reed?" Her eyes brightened, and she tapped his knee. "Oh, my. She was a few years ahead of me at Last Chance, wasn't she? She's such a lovely girl. A mother now, though, isn't she? With young boys."

The tears fell faster. "I would ruin them."

"Indeed, you would," she agreed, "if you hurt yourself now. But if you helped save the king, just think what you could offer them."

He looked over at her. "You don't understand…"

She smiled, and Flint thought he had never seen her look so beautiful. "Oh, from what Miss St. Clair has been saying about you and Mr. Harvester, I think I do. I'm sure Lord Flint does, and I haven't heard him say a thing against you—-well, except that you tried to shoot him."

Reed looked over at Flint. "I'm so sorry…"

Flint nodded. "I appreciate your missing."

The gun was beginning to droop. Flint balanced on the balls of his feet so he could move fast.

"This is a coward's way out, Francis," he urged. "And you are no coward. I served with you, remember? I know you. And I know that you don't want John Harvester's memory to be tainted by poisonous accusations. But John is gone. He doesn't care anymore. He died a hero trying to relieve my men. That is what we'll remember. I'll make sure of it."

The tears came fast now. "I…I loved him."

It was Flint's turn to nod, the fresh pain of still-new grief welling in his own chest. "He was a good man."

Reed's hand shook all the more, and Flint knew he was running out of time.

"Francis," he snapped, his voice sharp with well-remembered command. "We will protect you and yours. Drop. The. Gun."

It seemed to be working. The gun drooped. Francis lowered his hand.

Now! Flint jumped at him and grabbed it before Francis could change his mind.

But all the fight had gone out of the man. He merely dropped his head and closed his eyes as Flint secured the weapon and unloaded it for good measure before setting it on a table far away from Reed.

"Francis," he said, laying a hand on the man's shoulder. "I did not drag you out of that burning chapel to see you end like this."

The man sobbed. Felicity reached forward again and took a tight hold on one of Reed's hands.

Flint held onto Francis's shoulder. "The names on the list," he said.

Francis nodded. "All ripe for blackmail. Coercion

into treason."

"We shall try to protect them as well. Do you have names of the people who have pressured you?"

Francis nodded, his head down.

Flint turned back to see that Felicity's complexion had paled considerably, even as she continued to smile at that sad man. Miss Chase had her arm wrapped around Aunt Winnie's shoulder, still holding the old woman's hand. There were tears streaming down Winnie's cheeks as well. Flint wasn't quite sure what question to ask first.

"Are you all right, Felicity?"

She briefly looked at him, her eyes also awash in tears, and smiled for him. "Of course."

He nodded back, wondering at her immeasurable courage. "I know someone is going to tell me how this all came about."

He got vague nods.

"Francis wished to talk to me," Aunt Winnie said, suddenly looking her age. "He wanted to share some last words about John before he left. He has come for some time so I could hear of John and now, share...memories."

Flint stared at her and then Reed. "John Harvester? Why?"

It seemed they hadn't run out of surprises. Winnie straightened, still holding Miss Chase's hand as if it were a lifeline. "Because John Harvester was my son."

Flint found himself dropping into the settee next to Felicity. "I beg your pardon?"

For the first time in his life, he saw real despair in the old woman's eyes.

"Your grandmother protected me. Gave me a place when it became apparent that I...that..." She shook her head and gulped down a sob. "After John was sent away to be raised by the vicar and his family, I just...stayed." The tears were coming much faster now. "He never knew, of course. But Francis heré did. He kept me apprised of John's doings. He has been so very kind to me."

Flint felt as if he'd been bludgeoned. John Harvester. Laughing, brash, madly courageous John who had died in that fiery hell that was Hougoumont.

"Francis said that John died from a gunshot wound to the head," Aunt Winnie said, her eyes pleading. "Quickly, before he knew it."

Screaming, screams Flint would hear until the day he died. He swore his arm started burning all over again.

"Yes," he lied without blinking, because lies were the only comfort left. "He did."

And suddenly, Felicity was holding his hand. Not a gentle touch, a fierce grasp, as if she were holding him up away from that fire. As if she knew all of it. He looked over at her and saw the truth in her eyes. He wanted to feel ashamed. He had lost them all in that holocaust. His men. And yet reflected in her eyes was certainty, sympathy, sorrow.

She should have accused him. They all should have. And yet, somehow, she gave absolution. For the first time since June, the bands of suffocating guilt began to loosen, just a little.

And then something Winnie said struck him.

"John didn't know?" he asked her as gently as he could.

She lowered the handkerchief she had been using on her eyes. "Only your grandmother and the vicar knew."

Flint turned to Francis. "If John didn't know," he said, "how did you?"

He hadn't thought Francis could look worse. But one glance at Winnie had the man all but collapsing.

"They told you about John, didn't they?" Flint asked. "To get you inside the house."

Francis closed his eyes again. "They wanted to know about the various people the duke ran through here. Especially the girls."

Those vulnerable, frightened girls who had thought they were going on to safety. Oh, sweet God. "What did you tell them?"

Francis's smile was tragic. "The truth. That I saw no girls at all. I came to visit Winnie, and I made sure never to see any but regular staff." He shrugged. "It was an excuse to come. And I hurt no one."

That brought a bark of laughter from Aunt Winnie. "You mean those girls they traipsed through here they didn't want me to know about?" she demanded. "Fah! Of course, I knew. They were frightened enough without having to meet me. You've straightened that out with that pompous father of yours, I assume?" Flint was fast losing what equanimity he had left. "I did. You never mentioned them to Francis here?"

She glared at him. "Why should I? Not his business, was it?"

Flint almost smiled at that. Leave it to his Aunt Winnie to recover at double speed.

"You have the list, Flint," Felicity said. "And Mr. Reed didn't do anything else. You can help him, can't you?"

Flint squeezed her hand. "If I can't, the duke will."

"He will not," Flint heard from the open door and sighed. He should have known.

"He will," Flint said, not facing his father.

"And why should he, when you are attempting to cover up treason? Will there ever be a time you don't disappoint me?"

Flint was about to correct him when he lost hold of Felicity. Suddenly she was on her feet, bristling like a cat.

"Why, you vile old man," she snapped, her head back to meet the duke eye-to-eye, her hands clenched on her hips. "How dare you threaten him?"

The duke actually looked a bit taken aback. Flint was trying not to smile. Winnie looked like she had a box for a circus.

"And who are you to talk to me that way?" his father demanded of the woman who barely came up to his breastbone.

"I'm nobody," she assured him with a sharp tap to the chest. "But this nobody can see that you don't deserve a son like Flint. What have you done after all, to match his sacrifices? Or even, come to think of it, deserve them?"

Flint was on his feet now. She was about to get into trouble.

His father was pulling himself up to his formidable height and staring all the way down the ducal nose.

"You are speaking to a duke," he growled. "You

have no idea what responsibilities I have."

She waved a hand in his face. "Bah! Have you risked your life on a battlefield? Walked right into the killing fields of cannon fire or held for hours a walled enclosure that has been described as a holocaust? Do you even care that he bears scars from pushing his way into a blazing building to try to save his men from that hell? Have you lived every moment of your life since carrying the weight of the men you couldn't save? Have you ever once even asked what your son has sacrificed not only for his country and his men, but for you? How *dare* you belittle him, when I doubt you have so much as sacrificed your dinner to protect those you love."

Flint was absolutely frozen. She was punctuating each accusation with a finger jab into the ducal chest.

"He lied to you," the duke sneered down at her. "He was never to marry you. Why on earth would you defend him?'

She pointed in Flint's direction. "I would defend him for those scars he bears. I just cannot imagine why you do not."

"You don't think he should do his duty and marry you?"

Everybody in the room turned on her. She flushed.

"I am quite finished being anyone's *duty*," she said, and turned for the door. "There is a position waiting for me in Derbyshire."

Flint almost waited too long to catch hold of her. "Yes, there is. But it's not in that paltry school. Now, come."

"You're going nowhere," the duke barked, "Or I will not help this *friend* of yours."

Flint stopped, a struggling Felicity in his grasp, and bestowed a cold smile on his sire. "I wasn't speaking of you. I was speaking of Wellington. He values heroism and loyalty. Especially the kind of heroism that saved his own life. Besides, the House of Lords likes Francis better than you, too."

"You will not—"

"Enough!" Winnie suddenly barked. "I might enjoy a good dust-up on occasion, but this is beginning to bear all the hallmarks of a French farce. And since it is my room, I can toss the lot of you out. Except for Francis. Now, go. I need to talk with him."

"This is not *your* house, madame," the duke snapped.

"No," Flint agreed. "It is *my* house. Unless you want to take back your promise in front of witnesses."

Giving his father a gentle shove towards the door, Flint took better hold of Felicity's arm before she could protest.

"Now, Felicity," he said, meeting his fiancée's blazing glare, "you and I have a discussion to finish."

Flint gathered up the gun, handed it to the slack-jawed duke, and guided Felicity out the door. He had the most disconcerting feeling that he spotted a glint of humor in his father's eyes.

CHAPTER 15

W ELL, FELICITY THOUGHT SOURLY, AT least this time she wasn't under the bed. She had been plopped on top of it like an unwanted package.

"Now then," Flint snapped, slamming the door shut.

Felicity drew a shaky breath and pushed a hand against her stomach. "Do you have a chamber pot?" she asked.

He stopped and stared. "A what?"

She pressed her other hand against her mouth. "A chamber pot. A vase. Anything."

Flint's eyes widened, but he dropped to the floor and reached under the same bed she'd been crouched under not what, four days ago? He got the thankfully empty chamber pot to her just in time.

She didn't have much to lose, since she hadn't had her breakfast yet, but what little she did have ended up in the chamber pot, her stomach heaving relentlessly for far too long.

By the time she could chance straightening, Flint was seated alongside her, his arm around her shoulder.

"Here," he said, offering his handkerchief. "Start here."

Felicity accepted it and wiped her mouth with badly trembling hands. "Thank you. Sorry. I believe I have had one too many surprises today."

"You?" Flint echoed on a wry laugh. "I'll thank you not to pull a stunt like that again as long as I live."

She looked up. "I wasn't the one with the gun. He was waiting in my room."

Flint nodded. His left arm still around her, he reached over to brush the damp hair back from her face. His hand was shaking as badly as hers.

Before she could think better of it, Felicity caught hold of it and pressed it against her chest. "We're all safe," she said. "Breathe."

His chuckle was dust-dry. "I am here to comfort *you*, you little nodcock. Not the other way around."

"There is no rule that says we may not comfort each other."

Reaching for the chamber pot, he cast a wry look at her. "Are we finished here?"

She gratefully handed it over. "Your reflexes are excellent."

"Too much practice."

Setting the pan on the end table, he reached back around and gathered her into his arms. Felicity wanted to sob. She had never felt so warm, comforted or safe in her life. It wouldn't last, though. It had never been meant to last.

At least for this moment she could savor it. She could pretend that when she was frightened or sad or frustrated, she would always have Flint's arms to walk into, his chest to rest against, the steady thrum of his heart to beat against her ear.

"I cannot believe you did that," he whispered over her head, resting his cheek against her crown.

"Did what? I told you. Mr. Reed was waiting for me. Not the other way around."

"I'm talking about someone far more dangerous."

"Oh, the duke?" she huffed in outrage all over again. "He does not deserve you."

There was a pause, and then the returned rumble of his voice against her ear. "How did you know about Hougoumont?"

"If you remember, I mentioned that we followed all your exploits at school."

"Hougoumont happened in June. You've been out of school for three years."

"Anyone who followed news of the battle of Waterloo knows what a heroic stand the soldiers made there. Besides, one of my girls' brothers is in the Coldstream Guards."

"What is his name?"

"Fletcher. Lieutenant Harvey Fletcher."

"Gangly blond who laughs like a horse?"

She pulled her head back and grinned at him. "That is Lieutenant Fletcher to the life. You pulled him out of that barn, didn't you? He didn't talk about it much, but he had burns, too, and he thought you walked on water."

She saw Flint close his eyes and knew she had pushed him back into that nightmare. Lifting her free hand, she laid it against his cheek.

"If you had gone back in yet again, we would have lost you, too, and the men would have lost their leader. And then who knows what would have happened to the rest? You all saved the battle by holding Hougoumont."

And I would have never had the chance to know the man I love, she thought.

She knew better than to say it. Flint Bracken didn't need one more responsibility. It wouldn't hurt to lay her head against his chest for just a few more minutes, though, would it?

"I'm sorry," he said, surprising her right back to a position of staring up at him.

She couldn't help it. She brushed her hand against that stubbly cheek. "What in heaven's name for?"

He possessed quite an impressive scowl. If she hadn't been hurting so much, she would have been forced to grin at him.

"I'm sorry you had to hear that conversation in the library."

"Oh," she said with a wave of her hand, her head back down so he wouldn't see the truth in her eyes. "It wasn't a surprise. Not really. And I did get my job back."

"No, you didn't."

Her head shot up again, her stomach plummeting. "You mean you're about to break that promise as well?"

His smile was gentle. She tried to pull away, but he held on inexorably, with utmost care. "I never made that promise, if you'll remember. The duke did. I promised to marry you."

She huffed. "If you wish to be truthful, you didn't do that either. You simply said you wanted to. It's all right. I forgive you. You were caught in a vise by your father, your honor and your loyalty. After all, I very well could have been a spy, and I would do just about anything to stop someone who threatened my country—"

"Felicity."

"—and besides, there is this lovely house he was holding over your head, the beast—"

"*Felicity.*"

She couldn't so much as look at him. She needed to get away before he shattered her into irreparable shards.

"—but I'm feeling so much better now, and if I could just get a rinse of water—"

Before she could say another word, he had a glass in his hand and was holding it out to her, along with the much-abused chamber pot.

Because she figured she couldn't humiliate herself any more than she had, she rinsed her mouth and spit. As he accepted everything back, she tried to slide off the bed.

He was quicker than she was.

"You need to listen to me," he said, his eyes deadly serious, his hands empty of encumbrance.

She shook her head. "If you dare try to make up for what your father said—"

He sighed. "I'm not making up for anything. I'm…Oh, blast, it seems there is only one way to get through to you." And before Felicity could so much as move, he had her in his arms again and was kissing her. Not a sweet kiss, not a kind kiss, not a kiss goodbye. A fierce, shattering, consuming kiss that robbed her of every ounce of strength so that she had to hold on as tightly as he held on to her. She lost track of time and place and self, somehow disappearing into the heat of him, of arms that held her up away from every hurt and sorrow, all the loneliness and struggle that surely waited beyond his arms. For now, though, for now she would sink into his embrace like a drowning soul and gladly give up all just for the exquisite heat of his mouth against hers, the comfort of his arms enclosing her, the music of his groan as he lifted a hand to the back of her head and held on even more tightly.

And then, from one moment to the next, he had her cheek pressed against his shoulder, and he was trembling as badly as she.

For a long while the two of them just breathed, silent and trembling. Inevitably, though, she felt him smile. "She doesn't have a grave," he said.

That brought her head back so she could face him. "Pardon?"

It didn't help. She was already lost again in the sweet green of his laughing eyes, the hard-cut planes of his dear face. The scent of the outdoors and the night that was particularly his.

His smile broadened as he brushed that loose lock of hair back from her temple again. "Your grandmother. You swore on her grave. She doesn't have one. At least Uncle Andy's mother doesn't. Would you like to meet her?"

Felicity found herself blinking like a stunned calf. "I'm sorry..."

This time he brushed a gentle finger along her cheek, leaning even closer. "Your threat if I followed you. I thought I would do my best to protect my poor cods by informing you that I don't think a swear is valid if the thing you swear on is not available. Your grandmother is alive. Therefore, there is no grave to swear upon."

She became caught on the pertinent part of that ramble. "I have a grandmother?"

She knew her voice sounded unpardonably small. But the news flummoxed her. She simply did not know how to take it. Her whole life she had insisted that she had no interest in a family. Especially a family that had no interest in her.

"Do you think——-"

"That she knows about you? I doubt it. If she had, she undoubtedly would have descended on that school like the Furies and swept you away."

Felicity attempted a smile. "Is she a dragon as well?"

He laughed. "I believe she taught the other dragons. You'll like her. She will love you. You have her spirit."

Felicity closed her eyes, unwilling to take that step towards actual hope. She shook her head. "I think I shall put that revelation away for another day. This one has already been far too full."

Flint pulled her close again and she let him, because she simply didn't have the strength to resist. She wanted even a few more moments there.

"Felicity."

Still she kept her eyes closed. "*Shhhhhh*. Let me enjoy this a bit longer before I have to go."

She could feel him stiffen. "Go? Go where?"

"Where I belong."

It seemed that was the wrong thing to say. Suddenly he pulled away, his hands clamped around her arms, his expression fierce as he glared down at her.

"How many times must I tell you that I will not have that kind of talk? You belong here, Felicity Chambers. In this house, with me. With my staff who will surely revolt if I drive you away. With my Aunt Winnie, who will need your strength and certainty." Pulling her close, he rested his forehead against hers. "With me, Felicity, because even knowing I wasn't supposed to, I'm afraid I've fallen quite in love with you and cannot let you go."

She felt tears rise again. She battled the terrible pain of hope. "Why?" was all she could think to ask.

His laugh was breathless. "Damned if I know. All I know for certain is that if you leave this house, I must too. Because I cannot imagine living in it without you."

She lifted her head and met his gaze to see more than she ever could have hoped there. "Are you certain? This will annoy your father terribly, you know."

His grin was sudden and brash. "Yes," he agreed, "it will. Won't it?"

She pulled back a bit. "Is *that* what this is all about?"

He scowled. "Did that kiss feel as if my father was all this was about?"

She thought about it a moment and was forced to smile. "No. No it did not."

He nodded. "In fact, I have—" He reached into his pocket only to come up empty. "Blast. I must have dropped it when I caught sight of that tableau in Aunt Winnie's room. Wait right here—"

Felicity held on more tightly. "I don't think so. I believe whatever it is can wait a few moments more."

He tilted his head, his eyes sparkling, "Even if whatever it is involves emeralds and diamonds?"

Again, she made a show of thinking on it. "Even

then."

She kept her silence through another protracted kiss that left both of them breathless.

"However, I wouldn't wait too long. Aunt Winnie will walk off with it."

Aunt Winnie tried. But she was no match for a woman who had finally found a home for her heart, especially when the ring was accompanied by a broken gold chain holding a battered locket. The duke might have huffed several times when Flint finally slipped the square-cut emerald on Felicity's finger and kissed her, but his outrage seemed less than sincere. In fact, Felicity had the strangest feeling that this was the ending the duke had planned for all along.

She found that she didn't care. She was home.

EPILOGUE

"ARE YOU QUITE SURE ABOUT this?" Felicity asked, pausing yet again on the steps of the red brick townhouse on Grosvenor Square.

It wasn't a big house, but it was impressive, with stone pediments and four bays of sparkling windows. And it was on Grosvenor Square.

Laying a hand against her back to urge her forward, Flint chuckled. "Of course, I am. You might not want to meet her, but she wants to meet you."

"I didn't say that exactly..."

It had been only two weeks, during which her life had been completely upended. She was no longer a teacher, but a fiancée, a nascent Society lady with a burgeoning wardrobe, a new family she was still trying to acclimate to and a fiancé who seemed to fit her like a glove.

And now, she had a grandmother.

Drawing a deep, unsteady breath, she let Flint guide her through the black wrought-iron gate and onto the front stoop to be greeted by an open door and an absolutely precise butler, who bowed the perfect depth and greeted them with a sonorous voice.

"My lord, welcome," he intoned. "Miss Masterson."

Something else to get used to. A new name to go with her new wardrobe and fiancé. She had balked at first when her Uncle Robert, Uncle Andy's brother, had proposed officially adopting her. She *liked* her own name. She had wanted to keep it as something that was still completely her own. But the marquess had seemed so sincere, so heartfelt in his offer—and his wife so gentle—that she found she couldn't say no. So here she stood, officially known as Felicity Chambers Masterson, and she was still trying to make it fit.

Although as Flint had reminded her, she wouldn't really have to since in another three weeks she would be a Bracken.

"Miss Masterson," Flint said with a grin, "this is Parsons. Parsons, Miss Masterson."

"A pleasure, Miss."

Felicity couldn't tell if it really was, as was the way with all butlers, but she took him at his word. "I as well, Parsons."

"Your grandmother is waiting in the Great Salon," he said and turned to lead the way.

The news did not help Felicity's nerves. So, it wasn't to be a visit as much as an audience. Great salons tended to be the size of ballrooms and decorated to intimidate.

She could have told them all that they didn't need to go to extra lengths. She was already intimidated. There were cherubs on the arched ceilings of the entryway and Ming vases in the niches along the walls, a Rubens above the staircase and a Canaletto view of Venice along the hallway.

"I'd love to go there," she sighed, seeing it.

"On our wedding trip?" Flint asked.

She hadn't meant to say that out loud. She shook her head. "One thing at a time. This thing is my grandmother."

"Lord Flint Bracken," the butler intoned. "And Miss Masterson."

For the brief, breathless moment before she stepped across that threshold, Felicity held onto her all the uncertainties, the losses and yearnings and betrayals she had built up over the years, the family she had imagined and the one she had been given. And then, because she knew that, no matter what, he would be both of those things, she took tight hold of Flint's hand.

"Ready?" he whispered.

She nodded. "Ready."

And stepped into the room to be hugged by a weeping, white-haired woman who kept repeating her name as if it were a benediction. And behind her a room of people behind her who smiled in greeting.

Later Felicity would remember those moments as the greatest revelation of her life. Because in meeting the family she'd never thought to have, she made an even greater discovery. Even without them, with Flint she would have had family enough.

But it certainly was nice to have the rest.

OTHER TITLES BY EILEEN DREYER

BARELY A LADY

Olivia Grace has secrets that could destroy her. One of the greatest of these is the Earl of Gracechurch, who married and divorced her five years earlier. Abandoned and disgraced, Grace has survived those years at the edge of respectability. Then she stumbles over Jack on the battlefield of Waterloo, and he becomes an even more dangerous secret. For not only is he unconscious, he is clad in an enemy uniform.

But worse, when Jack finally wakes in Olivia's care, he can't remember how he came to be on a battlefield in Belgium. In fact, he can remember nothing of the last five years. He thinks he and Olivia are still blissfully together. To keep him from being hanged for a traitor, Olivia must pretend she and Jack are still married.

To unearth the real traitors, Olivia and Jack must unravel the truth hidden within his faulty memory. To save themselves and the friends who have given them sanctuary, they must stand against their enemies, even as they both keep their secrets.

In the end, can they risk everything to help Jack recover his lost memories, even though the truth may destroy them both?

"Readers will love the well-rounded characters and suspenseful plot, and will cheer on intelligent, resourceful Olivia and Lady Kate as they take on disparaging men, backstabbing relatives, and stealthy assassins."~ Publishers Weekly on Barely a Lady

"Barely a Lady is addictively readable thanks to exquisitely nuanced characters, a brilliantly realized historical setting, and a captivating plot encompassing both the triumph and tragedy of war. Love, loss, revenge, and redemption all play key roles in this richly emotional, superbly satisfying love story."~ Booklist, Starred Review

TWICE TEMPTED

Fiona Ferguson's troubles began with a kiss . . .
It feels like a lifetime ago that Alex Knight saved Fiona from certain doom . . . and stole a soul-shattering kiss for good measure. Wanting nothing more than to keep her safe, he left her in the care

of her grandfather, the Marquess of Dourne.

But Fiona was hardly safe. As soon as he could, the marquess cast her and her sister out on the streets with only her wits to keep them alive.

Alex has never forgotten that long-ago kiss. Now the dashing spy is desperate to make up for failing his duty once before. This time he will protect Fiona once and for all, from a deadly foe bent on taking revenge on the Ferguson line-and anyone who stands in the way . . .

"Eileen Dreyer has created excellent plotting, characterizations, and pacing of narrative. Ms. Dreyer presents the reader with an exciting, well written story of romance, spies, loyalty and betrayal."~ Fresh Fiction on Twice Tempted

SIMPLE GIFTS

Rock O'Connor is a burned-out cop who doesn't have time for perky artistic types without sense. Lee Kendall would much rather she never had to deal with him. But when she's hit by a car, she finds herself being stalked by criminals who want something she has. She never expects that in an attempt to save her life, she loses her heart.

"Dramatically moving and emotionally poignant"
~ Affair de Coeur

SOME MEN'S DREAMS

She has no time for love…

Dr. Gen Kendall has paid too high a price to let anything get in the way of her dream. In one month she'll be a full-fledged doctor. She just has to impress her chief of staff, Dr. Jack O'Neill. She impresses him, all right. With one swing of a softball bat she puts him in his own hospital and changes both of their lives forever.

He has no taste for love…

A widower with a 12-year-old daughter, Jack hopes this move to Chicago will signal a new life for them both. He doesn't plan on finding himself literally at the feet of one of the most compelling women he's ever known. He certainly doesn't expect her to turn his life upside down when she recognizes something in his daughter that could well break his heart. Is love enough to see them through, especially when it means that not just Jack but Gen must face the ghosts of their pasts to save his little girl?

ADDITIONAL TITLES FROM
EILEEN DREYER

Korbel Classics Collection
Jake's Way
Simple Gifts
Timeless
Perchance To Dream
A Soldier's Heart
A Rose For Maggie
A Walk On The Wild Side
Some Men's Dreams

Korbel Classics Humorous Collection
The Ice Cream Man
Isn't It Romantic?
A Prince of A Guy
The Princess & The Pea
A Fine Madness
Humorous Boxed Set

Drake's Rakes Series
Barely A Lady
Never A Gentleman
Always A Temptress
It Begins With A Kiss
Once A Rake
Twice Tempted
Miss Felicity's Dilemma

Other Regency Romance
Dueling with the Duke (featured in the Duke's
by the Dozen Anthology)

FREE SHORT STORY

THE COWBOY & THE FAIRY GODMOTHER

In 1937, Reno is the place to go for a divorce. It's the only reason Emily Shepherd has traveled there, to break free of her profligate movie star husband. Little did she know when she stepped off the train that destiny in the form of a plump little woman named Merryweather was about to take a hand.

Joe Manion is at the train station to pick up a horse. Merryweather wanted him to take home so much more. The question was, did he believe in fairy godmothers? And would he let her talk him into taking home so much more?

Claim your FREE copy : *BookHip.com/LDALVT*

ABOUT THE AUTHOR

New York Times Bestselling, award–winning author Eileen Dreyer has published 40 novels and 10 short stories under her name and that of her evil twin, Kathleen Korbel in contemporary romance, paranormal romance, historical romance, romantic suspense, mystery and medical forensic suspense. A proud member of RWA's Hall of FAME, she also has numerous awards from RT BookLovers and an Anthony nomination for mystery. She is now focusing on what she calls historic romantic adventure in her DRAKE'S RAKES series. A native of St. Louis, she still lives there with her family. She has animals but refuses to subject them to the limelight.

Made in the USA
Monee, IL
18 November 2019